Petteril's Time
Lord Petteril Mysteries, Book 1
Mary Lancaster

Petteril's Thief

Chapter One

T he small thief known as Ape froze in a sudden draught.

As though a window had suddenly blown open.

Abandoning the lantern and the calico bag into which he had been happily stuffing a roll of paper money and a few elegant sleeve buttons from the open safe chest, the boy crept out of the dressing room and into the main bedchamber. And his stomach seemed to lunge up into his throat.

One of the full-length French windows had indeed blown open, lifting the curtain and admitting a suddenly bright patch of moonlight. Through the glass, the thief could see the outline of a small, stone balcony and a man's tall, slender back.

Gawd All Mighty! How did I miss that cove?

The only thing to do was grab the bag, get out as fast as he could, and face Lord's temper at such meagre pickings. Except for some reason, there seemed more wrong here than an empty house that wasn't empty at all. The man on the balcony looked well dressed like any nob, and his profile was that of a young man. Yet his shoulders were stooped like someone old and weary, and he seemed to be swaying.

Gawd's bottom, is he bosky? Drunk enough to fall over the balustrade?

Heart in his mouth, Ape took a step closer, and then another. *I must be dicked in the nob...* He found himself almost at the window, but the man didn't seem to see or hear him. Worse, Ape recalled that they were three floors up, and here at the back of the house, the flag-stoned

1

yard directly below dipped even beneath the basement kitchen. If this drunken fool fell over, he would die.

And he was going to. He swayed toward the balustrade with such sudden force that Ape knew he would go straight over. Before he could stop himself, Ape dived out the window, grabbed the fellow's hand and hauled him back.

The drunk didn't even seem surprised. In fact, he seemed reluctant to turn his head, though he finally did, blinking at Ape as though not quite seeing him.

Well, if he's that jug-bitten, perhaps he won't remember me, Ape thought optimistically. For good measure, he hauled the man through the window, which he shut and locked.

The drunk, eerily illuminated in the shaft of moonlight through the glass, was still gazing at him, a faint frown forming between eyes that seemed to be gaining in focus. "Who the devil are you?"

"Who the devil are *you*?" Ape retorted, "Some drunk wandered in off the street? You want to go home, you do. You'll have a head thick as a turnip in the morning." Even as he said the words, it came to him that the man did not smell of drink. Nor, apart from the swaying, did he move like a drunk.

The man ambled past him, and Ape heard the sound of flint striking before the glow of several candles sprung up. Ape hadn't even seen the candle sticks. They were probably silver. Lord would want those.

"What you doing up here in the dark anyway?" Ape asked in severe tones as he backed toward the door. "Never tell me you own this ken?"

The man, who was tall and thin, his clothes decent if hardly the first stare of fashion, blinked at him. His face was handsome enough with its high forehead, long nose and well-defined bones, yet it looked sad and bleak to Ape. His shock of curly hair, the colour of chestnuts in autumn, was dishevelled and untidy. Even the dark, dark eyes held a hint of desperation, although Ape didn't know how they could give the impression of being both perceptive and utterly vague at the same time. The man turned his head, as though distracted, looking toward the dressing room where the lantern still shone on Ape's bag of meagre loot.

Hell and the devil! He'd nearly forgotten it. Hastily, Ape changed direction and swaggered toward the bag. "Well?" he said aggressively, referring to his last question in the hope of distracting his unwanted companion.

The man appeared to think about it. "It wasn't dark when I arrived," he said vaguely, while Ape swiped up the bag. "And yes, apparently so."

Ape knew better than to believe a word of it. "Well, stay away from windows till you're sober," he advised.

The faintest of smiles flickered across the man's face without lightening it in the least. "I don't suppose you found any brandy?" he said, nodding at Ape's bag.

Ape stopped swaggering, noting that the man now stood between him and the door. "No," he said brazenly. "Empty, dreary kind of place. Inhospitable."

"True," the man agreed. He held out his hand.

Ape looked at it, then at the man, sizing up his speed and strength. Not quick, he decided, not in this state, but definitely bigger than Ape. And in the way. "Split it with you?" he said hopefully.

The man said nothing. His hand remained steady.

With a sigh, Ape handed over the bag. "Lord's going to kill me now."

"The good Lord?" the man said, rummaging in the bag among the bits of lace, silk and linen without obvious interest.

"Nah," Ape said and decided, reluctantly, to scare off the gentleman. "He's a bowman prig, Lord is."

"Prig," the man repeated, more thoughtfully. "Thief? Burglar?"

"That's it. Powerful mean he is, too."

"You can't like working for someone powerful mean," the man observed.

"I don't," Ape admitted. "But a man has to eat."

His unwanted companion looked up from his haphazard poking about in the bag and examined Ape with the first glimmerings of real intelligence. "A man," he repeated. "How old are you?"

Ape shrugged. "Don't know."

"How'd you get in? Pick the lock on the back door?"

"Nah, we're not on the dub lay. Trigged the jigger yesterday, like, to see the place was empty, then milled the glaze on the pantry so I could wriggle in through the bars."

The gentleman regarded him with some fascination. His lips even twitched and there might have been some light in those bleak eyes. Ape felt ridiculously pleased.

"You didn't pick the lock," the man guessed. "I'm going to ignore the jigger and guess you broke the pantry window. You were sent inside to do the work while your Lord snoozes outside."

"He don't snooze," Ape said. "He looks out for the Watch, or anyone coming home."

"Slim pickings." The man let the bag dangle from his slender hand. "What's your name?"

"Ape. Won't do you no good. They'll never find me."

"Who won't?"

"The Watch! The Runners! Mister, are you dicked in the nob?"

Again, his lips twitched. "That one I know, and yes, probably." Unexpectedly, he tossed the bag to Ape, who only just caught it, and stepped aside. "Shab off, then."

Ape could not believe his luck and stared at the gentleman. He hadn't even taken the money from the bag, or the gold cuff links.

"Shab *straight* off," the man clarified.

"What are you going to do?" Ape blurted.

"Sleep," the gentleman said, and actually lay down on top of the bed.

Ape blinked at him owlishly for a moment, then went and blew out the candles before collecting his lantern and hurrying away. In the passage, he felt moved to close the door, and glanced first at the still, dark mound on the bed. He might already have been asleep.

Totally dicked in the nob. But he'd saved Ape a thrashing and so Ape would tell no one about his presence.

Piers Withan, fifth Viscount Petteril, woke slowly and reluctantly to daylight which pierced his eyes though not the blackness within him. Turning his back on the light, he closed his eyes again. Only, then he heard the unmistakable sound of a door closing.

The front door, by the sound of it.

Unlikely to be the return of the small burglar or even his "powerful mean" master. The footsteps on the stairs were stately but hardly stealthy, and he was sure he could make out the rustle of silk gown.

Piers swore beneath his breath and sat up. He was fully dressed but cold since he hadn't even pulled the dusty coverlet over himself. Stiffly, he eased himself off the bed and dragged his fingers through his hair.

At least he was standing when the interloper sailed into the room and came to an abrupt halt at sight of him. A rare squeak of alarm even escaped her lips.

The Dowager Viscountess Petteril was a severely handsome woman of middle years, as always dressed in the first stare of fashion without a hair out of place. She had a small, distinctive mole an inch from the corner of her mouth, which resembled the beauty patches worn by previous generations.

"Piers!" she uttered, her gloved fingers flying to her throat in alarm. "What on earth are you doing here?"

"Apparently, I live here. Among my other residences."

"Don't be obtuse, Piers. I mean you gave no one any warning you were coming. The house is hardly ready to receive you."

"The house and I are never likely to be ready for each other. Did you want something, aunt?"

A brief struggle waged across her face, then her chin came up. "Yes. I came for the Petteril necklace. I want Augusta to wear it next week at the Amberly ball." She looked down her nose at him, which was quite a feat when she stood a good ten inches shorter than he. "If you have no objection."

"Gussie?" Piers repeated in surprise. A vague memory of a lively tomboy child passed through his mind. "Is she out?"

"She is seventeen," Aunt Hortensia said sharply. "Of course, she is out. This is her first Season."

"Oh. Where is this necklace?"

"In the safe, of course."

There was no *of course* or indeed *safe* about it. No one had been living here for months and there had been at least one thief in here. On the other hand, there had been no necklaces in the child's bag of pilferings.

Piers waved her through to the dressing room and watched as she knelt by the empty safe. She found the spring without difficulty and opened the secret compartment, in which the true valuables had always been stored. Some fine pearls, an antique ring.

"Where is it?" Hortensia demanded.

"I don't even know *what* it is."

"Three strands of rubies set in gold! You will have seen me wear it several times."

"Then perhaps you still have it."

She glared at him with withering contempt. "They belong to the Petteril estate. Not to me."

Piers thought of the thief. It looked as if he hadn't found the secret compartment in the safe, for he hadn't taken the pearls or the ring. On the other hand... It was possible his master stole to order, and the order had been for the Petteril ruby necklace. Which would explain why there wasn't much else in the bag. Perhaps it had just been for show and quite unimportant. After all, the boy had almost left it behind.

"You know where it is," Hortensia accused.

"Perhaps. If I find it, I'll send it to you."

"You *must* find it. It is a valuable antique, a gift to the first Lord and Lady Petteril from Charles the Second, part of the estate that you will pass on to your heirs."

"I look forward to it."

Her sharp eyes narrowed. "I have never been sure you are not an imbecile, Piers. How in the world did you pass the entrance examinations to Oxford? I suppose your uncle spoke for you."

"I suppose he did," said Piers, who had not only two first class degrees but several years university teaching behind him.

Hortensia sniffed. "I must go. Don't forget." She spun on her heel, then turned back frowning. "You can't live here like this. There are no servants. You must stay at a hotel or somewhere while the house is made ready."

Piers dredged up his memory, for he had no intention of staying at a hotel. "What happened to the housekeeper? And the butler who used to be here? Harris? No, Herries."

A tinge of colour crept into Hortensia's perfect, pale skin. "They chose to come with me."

Piers smiled. "Of course they did. Leaving the house entirely unoccupied." Except by thieves.

Hortensia's nostrils flared. "I'll interview some servants for you and send them round within a day or so. You should stay at Grillon's until then."

"Please don't. I'll find my own servants."

She looked him up and down with weary scorn. "Piers, you can't even find your own clothes."

"Good day, aunt."

She looked slightly surprised by that, but since she obviously had nothing else to say and was indeed on her way out, she simply nodded curtly and walked away.

Piers watched her go without regret. He had never cared much for her, and she clearly despised him all the more for his recent elevation to her late husband's title. After all, if life had been fair, her son would have inherited. One of her sons. It would have been better for everyone, but life was rarely fair.

Most of his mind had already returned to the small thief. He even had a name, if only Piers could recall it... Monkey? Ape, that was it. There seemed to be very little reason in nicknames. But there had been intelligence and guile in that smooth young face with eyes as old as the hills.

Last night was mostly blackness for Piers. He doubted he'd have any chance at all of recognizing his thief, even if he found him among whatever slums or rookeries sheltered him. Dangerous places to go. But God knew Piers needed a purpose to get through the darkness and right now he didn't much care which end of that darkness took him. He would try.

He sat down on the edge of the bed, and after a few moments emitted a small, harsh laugh. *Why not? Why in hell not?*

Hortensia, Dowager Lady Petteril, left her old home rather faster than she had entered it so blithely only minutes before. Unaccountably ruffled by her encounter with her husband's nephew, she was conscious largely of grief and alarm.

Since she had not troubled to take the carriage, she walked straight round to Mount Street, where resided her elder, married daughter Maria, Lady Gadsby.

Maria was discovered writing letters in the morning room, though she looked up quickly when her mother was announced. "Mama. You are abroad early."

"Not early enough," Hortensia said grimly. "Where is Jeremy?"

"In bed. He never rises before eleven."

On a good day. "Did he take the necklace?"

"What necklace? Take it where?"

"The Petteril necklace, of course."

There was a short silence. "Don't be silly, Mama," Maria said impatiently. She had already returned her attention to her letter.

"It's gone," Hortensia informed her. "And Piers is in residence."

At that, Maria's pen paused. Her back was rigid with disapproval. She placed her pen in the stand and finally turned in the chair to face Hortensia. "Is he indeed? I expect he took it then. Why do you care? It's his now, and it's not as if any of us actually likes it."

"It is worth a fortune."

Maria stared at her in sudden indignation, her colour suddenly high. "So you assume Jeremy took it? Perhaps he staked it in a casual card game!"

Annoyed, Hortensia felt a faint flush rise to her own cheeks. "You have grown sarcastic since your marriage. It is not an attractive trait. Of course, I did not imagine anything of the kind, but if he has borrowed it for any purpose, I need to know."

"How could he even get in? The house is locked up and I gave you the keys back days ago. If you really think someone broke in and took it, try my cousin Bertie. It is he who bears quite the grudge about Piers inheriting the title."

"Perhaps I shall send a note round to him," Hortensia said thoughtfully, for though Bertie was the son of her husband's youngest brother, he was several years older than Piers, the son of the middle brother. And Bertie resented the fact, quite vocally on occasion. "Call this afternoon and we shall discuss it. Bring Jeremy."

"I can't this afternoon, Mama. I'm promised to Caroline Jeffries."

Hortensia frowned. "I cannot like Mrs. Jeffries. I wish you would not spend so much time with her."

"Don't be silly, Mama, she is received everywhere. You would like her if you had ever met her."

"Oh, I have met her," Hortensia said. She had to bite her lip, to remind herself that there was really no crisis. Even the necklace was Piers's problem and yet stupid tears threatened. Nothing had gone right since poor John's death in Portugal. Since then, she had buried her other son and her husband, and it seemed that only anger kept her alive.

"I have not laid eyes on Piers in five years or more," Maria said, deliberately changing the subject, Hortensia suspected. "What is he like now?"

Hortensia curled her lip. "Just the same. Stupid. Helpless. Annoying."

Maria smiled. "Mama, he cannot be stupid—"

"In any sense that matters to us, he is," Hortensia maintained. "Completely lacking in understanding, social grace, manners, quickness of wit..."

"I remember him being quite quick," Maria said, frowning as though in an effort of memory. "And funny, actually. There was one day we were all at Petteril House, dressing up in the attic and rehearsing this silly play we had made up. Piers actually seemed to turn into his character, had us all in stitches..." Her smile faded. "Until George realized he wasn't the centre of attention and the play got lost."

"Well, Piers is certainly the centre of attention now," Hortensia said with contempt. "I doubt it will work out well for him."

Chapter Two

Ape had sustained only one blow from Lord, mostly because he had dodged the rest with quick footwork.

"Is that all?" Lord had demanded in disgust. "Word I heard, there's a chest full of jewels in there!"

"I found the chest," Ape had assured him, ducking, "but it had only a bit of paper money and sleeve buttons. They're pretty enough." He had ducked and side-stepped the burglar's renewed fury. "There's china and glass and all sorts in there, too, but it'd break shoving it through the bars."

Lord had lunged at him, and Ape had taken off like a hare to avoid serious harm.

With no payment for his labours, he had found his way back to the Silver Jug. Lord would find him there if he wanted him, but hopefully not until his temper cooled.

Of course, Tatty the alehouse keeper was a touch ready with his fists, too, but at least he supplied food and the odd coin and even let Ape bed down in a corner of the room when the customers had gone.

Having glimpsed his face in the pewter mug—the one that masqueraded as the silver jug of the house's name—Ape used his finger to tug his tangled hair over the bruise now ripened on his cheek. He didn't want to inspire anyone to belt him on the other side. He swept the floor as he was told, shovelling out the filthy old sawdust and spreading down fresh stuff from the bucket at the back door.

Tatty vanished into the backroom with one of his furtive kind of customers, leaving Ape to finish with the sawdust and serve any early drinkers. Neither of them expected any, for most of Tatty's clientele consisted of those who preferred the dark. However, just as Ape shoved the bucket of sawdust aside, a stranger entered.

He was a small man, with a mean look in his eye, but around St. Giles, most people learned that kind of look as a protection if nothing else, so Ape thought nothing of it.

"What can I get you, Mister?" he asked.

"Tatty."

"He'll be out in a minute. Got a bit of business to take care of. Ale while you wait?"

The man grunted by way of assent, so Ape poured him a mug of ale and carried it to the rickety table where the customer had sat down. Ape knew the table of old so was careful not to spill a drop as he placed it carefully.

However, he reckoned without the little man grabbing him by the free arm. With an entirely involuntary jerk, Ape flinched back, knocking over the ale which splashed off the table into the customer's lap. The customer leapt up with a curse and shoved Ape so that he fell backward, tripped over a stool and fell onto his rear-end.

"Little varmint, you did that deliberate!"

"I did not!" Ape protested, skittering back toward the wall, as the man came at him fists raised. "Shouldn't grab at a man like that!"

"You won't live to be a man," the man snarled, but unexpectedly a stick was jabbed into his chest.

"Tsk-tsk," tutted someone. "Never beat the staff."

Ape blinked up at a tall, thin man in spectacles. He had ink stains on his cuffs and his soft fingers, and despite the jabbing stick, he smiled with mild friendliness. He looked like a harmless clerk, possibly one who moonlighted as a forger. All the same the stick kept pushing at the smaller man until he fell back, and Ape scrambled to his feet. Only then did Ape trouble to peer more closely at his saviour—and his mouth fell open.

It was the man from last night who'd let him keep the loot and then gone to sleep on the bed. But there was something very different about him now. He didn't even sound the same. The plummy speech had gone, along with the vague, distracted manner. His eyes, behind owlish, wire spectacles, were direct and unafraid.

"Go," this man urged with a last shove of his stick. "Sit, and the boy'll bring you another mug. Suggest you don't grab him this time. Bring me one too, if you would," he added to Ape, and strolled over to the other table.

The small man eyed him with some doubt, but did as he was bidden, even if he wasn't sure why. Ape hastened to refill the fallen mug, and another for the clerk or whoever he was from last night.

"Have one yourself," his saviour suggested.

Ape never turned down any means of filling his belly, so served the small man first and then brought two other mugs over to join the mysterious man from last night.

His companion blinked at him, which at least looked comfortingly familiar. "Can't see a damned thing through these," he said, pushing the spectacles further up his nose. His plummy accent was back, too. "They're for reading."

Ape stared. "Then what you wearing them for?"

The man's eyebrows flew up. "Disguise, of course."

"Well, it's rubbish."

"No, it isn't. Took you a good half minute to spot me and it's only hours since you saw me."

Ape let that one go. "How'd you find me?"

"A bit of luck—almost tried the docks first, then decided on St. Giles since it's closer. Lots of people know a boy called Ape who works for a bowman prig called Lord."

Ape shut his mouth. Again. Then: "Why'd they tell you? You bribe them?"

"Said I had something for you to do. After several false starts, I was eventually directed here with the threat that one Tatty would garotte me if I meant no good."

"Tatty wouldn't garotte anyone," Ape scoffed, and took a mouthful of ale. "Though his brother might, I suppose."

"I am duly warned."

"What d'you want me to do, then?" Ape asked curiously.

The man took a mouthful of ale, and grimaced. "Give me back the necklace. Or tell me where to find Lord."

"What necklace?" Ape asked with a frown. "You mean from that ken last night? No necklaces there, though Lord was mad as fire because he'd heard there was good pickings—jewels and that."

The man set down his ale and made to rise. "Then take me to Lord."

"I ain't going near him for a week!" Ape said in some alarm.

The man's eyes pinned him to his seat. "Because he gave you that bruise?"

Ape grinned cheekily. "Dodged the rest and ran." He sighed. "Didn't get paid, though. That gaffe was a waste of time." Last night, there had been no sign of such a penetrating stare, as if the man's eyes skewered him to the seat while rummaging in his brain. "Whose is it, anyway?"

"Mine."

Ape frowned. "You don't look very pleased about it! Great big house like that."

"I don't mind the house. It's the trouble that goes with it that...annoys me."

"What, like me cracking it?" Ape asked uneasily.

Something that might have been laughter caught in the man's throat and died. "The least of it, I assure you. But you can still take me to Lord."

"He ain't got the necklace, mister, I swear."

"Were you meant to look for it?"

"He don't tell me stuff like that. Just get to the biggest bedroom at the back of the house, find the safe in the dressing room off it and bring him that and anything ese. Couldn't find nothing worth having so nabbed some silk clouths and lace bedcovers and everything in the safe chest—which weren't even locked, by the way, and no wonder. All I got from it were two pair of sleeve buttons, a tie pin and a roll of soft."

The man sighed. "Why do I believe you?"

"Swear on my blessed mother's grave," Ape said piously. "I never lie."

The man eyed him over his mug. "Where is your mother?"

"Gone to a better place," Ape said, gazing upward.

"Liar."

Ape grinned and shrugged. "Don't know. I look after myself."

"Do you know who directed Lord to my house?"

"Course not. He wouldn't tell the likes of me that."

"Suppose I'd better go and ask him, then." This time, he really did stand up, and Ape watched him with some disquiet.

For some reason, he felt responsible for the man. "You don't know where to find him."

"Queen's Head's a good start, I'm told."

Ape blinked with some respect. "Blimey. You do ask around."

"I'm good at questions." He frowned. "Will Tatty and his murderous brother really look after you?"

Ape thrust up his chin. "Told yer. I look after myself. I'm big enough and ugly enough."

The man gazed at him, then dropped a couple of coins on the table and turned away. "I suppose you know where to find me."

He really was going, Ape realized, and bolted after him in alarm. "What, you *really* going to Lord?"

The man glanced back over his shoulder. "Yes."

Ape swore fluently for several seconds under the gentleman's admiring gaze. Then he flung himself across the floor in front him. "Going out, Tatty!" he yelled, and stomped out of the alehouse.

Ape walked quickly and purposefully along the narrow street, the gentleman, whoever he was, swinging along at his side. The man seemed to follow his nose, but with no sense of danger, for twice Ape had to stop him turning up blind allies where the buildings on either side almost met in the upper storeys, and lurking, desperate people would happily leave you dead for the coins in your pocket.

"Do you even know where the Queen's Head is?" Ape asked irritably at last.

"No."

"Then how'd you plan to get there without me?"

"Same way I found the Silver Jug. Ask."

Ape glared at him. "You'll get your throat slit if you're not careful." All the same, he was actually secretly impressed by the gentleman. He might not have known which places to avoid at all costs, but somehow, as the ragged clerk, he managed to blend into his surroundings, almost as if he belonged. His shoulders were slightly hunched in a downtrodden way, yet his eyes were watchful and his step quick, as though he knew where he was going and why. He might have been a completely different man from the one who had almost swayed off the balcony to his death last night.

At the Queen's Head, Ape paused. "You sure about this, mister? Why don't I ask for you, whatever it is you want to know?"

"He might bruise the other side of your face."

Ape flushed with shame. "That's between him and me. I'm useful to him. You ain't. He'll do worse than backhand you."

The gentleman regarded him, his face unreadable. "Thanks for showing me the way. You can go back now."

The cool metal of a coin slid into Ape's hand. He wasn't daft enough to give it back, but he glared at the idiot who paid it. "I ain't finished with you yet," he said and barrelled into the tavern.

Despite its grand name, the front room of the house was dark, dingy and as grimy as the Silver Jug. The back rooms were more opulent and upstairs even more so, but Ape avoided going up there when he could.

He swaggered up to the potman. "Where is he?"

The potman nodded toward Lord's favourite back room. "I wouldn't. He ain't pleased with you."

"I ain't pleased with him," Ape retorted. "Who's with him?"

"Just Jakie."

It was probably as good a time as any, then. And Ape had the escape route planned in his head.

The potman cast a quick dubious look at his companion, but Ape knew better than to explain or excuse. Without looking at the gentleman, he strode up to the relevant door, bashed it once with his knuckles and walked in.

The room smelled of spirits and tobacco and rancid male sweat. Lord, his hat pulled down over his forehead, sat with his boots up on the table. Beside him was Big Jakie, idly shuffling a pack of cards. Two mugs and a jug of ale sat between them on the table, along with a labelless bottle.

"Look what the cat dragged in," Lord said sourly to Ape. "I got nothing for you. You're useless."

"Actually, it is I who have something for you," the gentleman corrected, never knowing, it seemed, when to keep his mouth shut. Another change had come over him, though. He spoke like someone trying to ape his betters. Yet his shoulders were straight and his eyes direct, like a man who feared nothing and held considerable authority.

Lord laughed, looking him up at down. "Who the blazes are you? And what could you possibly have that I want?"

The gentleman pulled up a chair and sat down uninvited—far enough from Lord's boots, at least, to be safe. "Coin. In return for information."

Lord laughed again, but Jakie sat up, staring at him. "Here, you ain't one of them Runners from Bow Street?"

"Would I bring a Runner here?" Ape demanded indignantly.

Lord sneered. "Gawd knows what you'd do, stupid little—"

"I represent," the gentleman interrupted, "one Lord Petteril."

That got their attention. They all stared at him. It seemed a mere matter of habit when Lord said, "No you bloody don't."

"His lordship wishes to know who sent you to burgle his house. He is prepared to pay."

Lord curled his lips into a familiar snarl. "I might be prepared to take it. From you. Before Jake here slings your body into the back sewer."

"I never heard you were so slow on the uptake, Mr. Lord." The gentleman sounded disappointed. "We imagined you would be as upset as his lordship by the failure of last night's robbery. His lordship not liking broken windows and kids running loose about his house while he's trying to sleep. And yourself, I had so foolishly thought, not liking to be sent on a wild goose chase for ruby necklaces that aren't there."

Ape held his breath, poised to grab the gentleman and run. Though God knew what he'd do after that. Lord offered the only possible way he could see out of this life, and Ape wasn't sure how much he could stand of the Silver Jug. But still, Ape had brought the gentleman here and was responsible for him.

Lord had gone very still, but he no longer sneered. "Where is it?"

"Who sent you to take it?"

"No one sent me!" Lord said angrily. He tugged his ear. "Overheard a conversation about an empty house and unguarded jewels. I'm me own man. So where is it?"

"That," the gentleman said, rising to his feet, "is what we would all like to know." He dropped a small, string-tied purse on the table. "Good day." He walked unhurriedly to the door—wouldn't do to bolt now.

But Lord couldn't rest if he wasn't master of any scene. He pocketed the purse quick as a heartbeat, and jerked his head at Jakie, who lurched with impressive speed to block the exit.

Ape's heart leapt into his mouth. Now he'd need to plead with Lord and promise him God knew what...

The gentleman did not break his stride. He simply brought up his stick smartly between Jakie's legs. Jakie howled and doubled up, while the gentleman eased him to one side with the stick and opened the door. Ape yanked it shut behind them on Lord's startled cursing.

"Don't stop," Ape said grimly.

But the gentleman did not hurry. And after a moment, Ape realized why. Neither Lord nor Jakie would ever speak of this, let alone admit it to the shadowy drinkers who must never know that a run-down clerk had defeated them so easily and so contemptuously. Lord needed respect.

But outside the tavern, the gentleman snatched off his glasses, stuffing them in his pocket, and walked so rapidly that Ape had to trot to keep up with him. He avoided the blind alleys this time, heading as if by instinct out of St. Giles. Ape thought he was frightened—until he glanced anxiously up at his face and saw the man was smiling.

Chapter Three

I n fact, Piers was exultant. It was like besting his cousins, without the emotional hurt. In fact, for Ape's sake, he wished it was Lord who had blocked his way.

Glancing down at Ape who was trotting along beside him, staring at him, he hastily wiped the smile off his face and asked, "Do you believe him?"

Ape blinked. "About overhearing a conversation rather than being sent to your ken? Prob'ly. It would explain why the facts was wrong."

"And why he didn't know about the safe," Piers murmured.

"He did know about that. He told me where to find it."

"But not how to get into it. He didn't even think it worth coming in himself. Wouldn't you normally have let him in through the door after you climbed in the window?"

"Maybe," Ape replied cautiously. He scowled. "You mean, he didn't want to risk himself on dodgy information?"

"Seems likely."

"It does," the boy allowed. They were emerging from St. Giles into wider streets, heading in the general direction of Oxford Street. "Where we going?"

"Hungry?"

"Starving."

"Me, too. This will do." He stopped at an unpretentious inn, where he could vaguely recall dining in the past and raised his hand to the door before he saw that Ape was hanging back. "What? You don't care for the food here?"

Ape scowled. "Ain't never eaten it and I don't know what you're up to neither."

Young face and old eyes. When he'd spilled the ale in the Silver Jug, it had been because the dirty little man had touched him. God knew what the child had suffered and what he had every reason to fear. But at least he hadn't bolted.

"I'm up to dinner," Piers said indifferently. "But I can dine alone if you prefer."

Ape stared at him, then dropped his eyes and shrugged. "I don't mind," he said and swept past him into the inn, both hands dug deep into his ragged pockets.

Piers's lips twitched as he followed.

Dinner was a very tasty beef and ale pie, with lots of gravy and potatoes and vegetable. Ape shovelled it in as if afraid it would be taken away from him at any moment. His table manners were non-existent, but then when survival took up all your time, when could he have learned?

"Why do you work for Lord?" Piers asked. "Does he force you?"

"Nah." Ape sat back on the bench and held his stomach with both hands. "I offer."

"You'll get caught. And he'll let you take the blame and do his time in Newgate."

"I know. Well, I won't be working for him again anyway. *You* saw to that."

"Sorry. Probably best."

"Prob'ly," Ape agreed, though there was a hint of regret, even loss in his voice.

"What will you do?"

"Go back to the Silver Jug. Tatty's not so bad."

"Then why go to Lord in the first place?"

"Way out," Ape said.

"Of St. Giles?"

"Everyone tells me no one ever leaves, but some do. Annie from the Queen's Head did—it's a bawdy ken, in case you didn't know. Annie's got a flash little place of her own now, all respectable like."

Piers latched on to the salient point. "You want to be respectable."

"Yes, but not like Annie." Colour seeped into his cheeky face. Beneath the grime, it was a likeable face, small features, wide mouth, impudently turned-up nose. Big, clear, blue eyes of an unusual shade, eyes that had seen far more than most people could imagine in their nightmares. "If a gent like you gets my meaning."

Piers met Ape's gaze with great care. "I imagine so. Not sure burgling houses with Lord is very respectable either."

"No, and I'd never save up enough of my share for a house like Annie's anyway, but maybe I could pay for a reference and get a job in a stable or somewhere. Become a groom."

"You like horses?" Piers asked, surprised.

"Like all animals. Tatty don't want me to feed the stray dogs, though, and he says the cats won't catch the mice if we give them anything else to eat."

"I'm surprised he cares. About the mice."

"He don't. He's just stingy." He grinned at Piers, who found himself smiling back.

"Apple pie?" the waitress offered cheerfully, collecting their empty plates.

"Cor," Ape said in wonder.

"If you please," Piers replied for them both. When she had bustled away again, he said, "You wouldn't be able to steal in a respectable position. You'd get dismissed and probably arrested."

"I know. I'm pretty poor at the diving anyway, even the clouthing lay, although I got a few."

The boy's language was ever intriguing. "You're not good at picking pockets?" Piers hazarded. "Even of handkerchiefs."

"Got taught as a kid but I ran away."

Piers blinked. "You've crammed a lot into a short life so far. Who would you pay for a reference for this stable job?"

Ape shrugged again. "I don't know. Someone like you, maybe." He grinned. "Someone you look like in that rig anyway. But you're out of twig, ain't you? You were *in* twig last night."

While their apple pie and custard was delivered, along with a jug of thick, fresh cream, Piers watched Ape's awe and interpreted his last comments to mean Ape knew he was in disguise today.

"A bit," he said, as Ape fell on his apple tart with delight. "Constantly out of twig nowadays. On the other hand, I do happen to know that Lord Petteril is hiring staff."

Ape's eyes widened. "Friend of yours?" He swallowed the rest of the food in his mouth and leaned his head thoughtfully to one side, no doubt thinking of the empty house that Piers had already admitted to owning. "Nah. That's you, ain't it?"

"It is," Piers admitted.

Ape grinned. "An actual lord?"

"Trust me, everyone finds it as bizarre as you do."

"Oh, *you* ain't bizarre," Ape assured him. "Well, maybe you're bit odd for a lord, though I've never met any before. But just imagine me eating apple tart with an actual lord!"

Piers's smile was crooked. He ate half of his own pudding and shoved the plate aside. Ape was watching him almost anxiously.

"Do you mean it?" the boy blurted.

"Mean what?"

"That you'd let me work in your stable?"

"If you understand that if you steal from me or anyone else, I'll dismiss you."

Ape's eyes fell. He laid down his spoon beside the bowl. "I did, though, didn't I?" he said bleakly.

"What, a few old handkerchiefs and pillowcases, and someone else's sleeve buttons? I gave them to you, if I recall. Even Lord's welcome to them."

Ape dashed the back of his hand over his eyes, then stared at him defiantly, daring him to notice. "Not the point, is it?"

"No, it's not the point," Piers allowed. "But it's different now."

"How?"

"I'm trusting you with my horses, and you're trusting me to pay you a fair wage."

"How much?" Ape demanded.

Piers frowned. "Actually, I don't know. I always looked after my own horse. Whatever the going rate is. I'll tell you this afternoon. Are you going to eat the rest of that tart?"

Ape eyed it doubtfully. "Will there be supper?"

"There will be supper."

"Cor. Then I probably don't have room. Where we going now?"

Piers counted some coins on to the table. "To Petteril House, where I shall introduce you to my horse. Then, you can muck out his stable while I make a very belated call upon my solicitor."

Piers left Ape in the mews stable, stroking the Professor's nose with a rather touching mixture of reverence and delight. Having introduced him to a couple of the other grooms in the mews—to make sure they understood that so disreputable looking a lad really did work for Viscount Petteril—he walked up to the house through the back garden.

Forcing himself, he paused to look at the cellar yard where he might so easily have splattered his brains last night, then up to the bed chamber balcony and window.

No more, he told himself. *Make the best life you can.*

His life had already taken a strangely intriguing turn, with the advent of Ape and the missing necklace. Small purposes, perhaps, but they were a beginning and he clung to that.

Washed and changed back into his normal if unfashionable clothing, he walked to Bond Street, picked a tailor at random, and had himself measured for new coats, pantaloons, breeches, and shirts, and asked for them to be sent around with cravats and under-linen to Petteril House as soon as each garment was ready. He then took a hackney to his solicitor's office in the City.

Here, he discovered Mr. Pepper of Pepper, Pepper and Patterson, delighted to take his instructions and explain the manner in which the estate had been left to him.

"Attention is necessary, my lord, I cannot deny it. The country estates, the household, the family allowances, all must be regularized, and coin must be spent. However, the Funds will keep us going until your lordship is back on your feet."

"Back on my feet?" Piers repeated uneasily. "Are you saying my finances are a shambles?"

Mr. Pepper permitted himself a small smile. "Not that, my lord, not yet. But it is undeniable that with so many months with no hand on the reins, as it were, and before that with Mr. George and then his lordship so ill..."

"You mean I should have stepped up to my duties months ago," Piers said flatly.

"You are here now," Mr. Pepper said kindly if evasively. "I understand you are in need of a full household staff. Would you like us to take care of that and send you the likeliest candidates for butler and housekeeper? Or shall I send them to them to her ladyship as she requested?"

Piers's eyebrows flew up. "Did she, by God? No, send them to me, if you please. As a matter of interest, who else has keys to Petteril House? Apart from myself and her ladyship?"

"Her ladyship gave her keys to me when she removed from Petteril House to her new establishment on Half Moon Street."

"Did the housekeeper do likewise when she removed with her ladyship to Half Moon Street?"

"Not to me, my lord."

"I suppose the butler had keys, too? I wonder who has those?"

"I'm sorry, my lord. It's a little ramshackle for my liking, but I suppose with so much tragedy and resulting chaos... Would you care to have the locks changed?"

Piers blinked. "What an excellent idea. Send me a locksmith tomorrow morning, if you would be so good."

Mr. Pepper beamed as though he had been granted a special favour. "Now, my lord, allow me to show you the accounting of all who have been drawing on the estate in your name since his late lordship passed away..."

Mucking out the stable—in many ways more pleasant than sweeping out the Silver Jug—didn't take Ape long, even stopping periodically to talk to the other grooms and stable lads in the mews. They all seemed very curious about his master and, rather to his surprise, didn't even sneer at Ape. After all, he might have been the lowliest of stable lads, but he worked for a lord, a viscount, which none of the others did. Plus, Petteril House was the largest on the square.

Ape didn't know much about grooming a horse, but after observing the others in the mews, he found the correct brushes in the stable and began to brush down the Professor. The horse seemed to like it as much as Ape did and nudged him with his nose whenever he could.

He was chatting away to the horse when a shadow fell over him. Instinct made him spin around, his heart lunging, ready to run or fight. An elegant stranger in the smart, scarlet uniform of a soldier and very splendid side whiskers regarded him from the doorway.

"God's little fishes," drawled this vision. "Who are you?"

"Stable lad to his lordship," Ape said at once. "Who are you?"

The magnificent soldier looked amused. "Cousin to his lordship. Where is he?"

"Out."

"Either that or he's hiding. When is he due back?"

Ape, whose hackles rose at the casual contempt in the soldier's voice as much as his words, merely shrugged. "Couldn't say."

The soldier's eyes roamed over the Professor. "Decent horse," he said as though surprised.

Ape made no comment.

The soldier began to turn away. "Well, if you glimpse the elusive viscount, you might tell him I came by."

"Can't, sir."

The soldier turned back, eyeing Ape with a mixture of fascination and distaste. "Can't, boy? You appear to have a tongue in your head. You're certainly insolent enough with it."

"Don't know who you are," Ape said flatly.

The soldier's lips curved. "Captain Withan."

Captain Withan strolled away, and Ape turned back to the horse, scowling. He didn't want *him* to have cousins like that.

He had brushed every bit of the Professor whose eyes had begun to hold a hint of accusation, when Lord Petteril himself strolled into the stable, a parcel under one arm. The Professor whinnied in recognition, thrusting his head at the viscount.

Ape grinned. "He's missed you."

"He's missed his oats," Lord Petteril said drily, and showed him how much to feed the horse at a time. After that, he cast an eye about the stable, much to Ape's anxiety, and then nodded. "Good. Well done. Now, shut him in and come up to the kitchen."

Ape brightened. "Is it time for supper?"

Petteril paused in the doorway. "No, but I suppose I'll have to think about it. There might be tea."

"Cousin of yours turned up," Ape said, trotting beside him through the garden to the kitchen door. "Soldier. Full of himself."

"Ah. Bertie."

"Captain Withan."

"What did he want?"

"He said to tell you he had come by."

His lordship grunted and unlocked the back door. Ape, interested to see the kitchen in the daylight, followed him inside.

"He said something odd. Said you were either out or hiding."

"Why is that odd?" His lordship dropped his parcel on the kitchen table, and, somewhat to Ape's surprise, set about lighting the large stove.

"How could he know you were out if he hadn't been into the house?" Ape said.

Lord Petteril straightened and glanced at him thoughtfully, before he picked up a kettle, which he filled with water from a tap over a large sink.

Ape sat down at the table. "Some of the other lads in the mews were talking to me. According to them, no one's lived here for months, but people keep coming and going. Apart from me and Lord, that they don't know nothing about. Strikes me any of those people might have taken this necklace of yours."

"Sadly, you are correct. I suspect the entire family have keys and wander in whenever they like for whatever purpose they like."

"What you going to do about it?" Ape asked severely.

"Change the locks."

It struck Ape, who had no time for family, that Petteril might be hurt by the behaviour of his. But then he suspected everything hurt his lordship, though no one else would ever see it. And Ape would never tell.

Lord Petteril sat down opposite Ape and shoved the parcel toward him. "I found you these."

Ape's eyebrows flew up. "What?"

"See for yourself."

Ape carefully untied the string and unwrapped the brown paper to reveal a jacket, two pairs of breeches, stockings, even underwear and new thick cotton shirts. Ape swallowed. Gratitude warred with fear.

"I got clothes," he muttered.

"Held up with string and far too big for you. I can't have servants dressed like that. Reflects badly on my standing."

Ape looked at him sharply, for a kind of bitter self-mockery had crept into his speech.

His lordship's eyes fell, as though he hadn't expected Ape to notice. "Also, you can work better without having to hold up your trousers with one hand."

Ape eyed his new apparel with continued doubt. "Thank you," he said dully.

Lord Petteril scowled, clearly expecting a fight. "And while we're on the subject, you still smell of the Silver Jug. You need a bath. With soap."

Ape felt suddenly breathless with delight. "Truly?"

Lord Petteril peered at him. "You *want* a bath?"

"Does the soap smell good?"

"Better than old beer and horse dung."

Ape grinned. "When can I bath?"

"When you've helped me heat the water and we've had a cup of tea."

It wasn't until later, when they were pouring buckets full of water into the tub in the corner of the kitchen that the suspicion struck Ape like a blast of ice-cold water.

"Here, you ain't going to be here while I take this bath, are you?"

Petteril shuddered in an exaggerated way that made Ape relax and grin. "Most assuredly not. I'm going to find somewhere to work upstairs. When you're clean, put on the new clothes and come and find me."

Captain Albert Withan of the Life Guards, known to his intimates as Bertie, was enjoying a late and largely liquid luncheon at White's, when he caught sight of his cousin Maria's husband, Jeremy Gadsby, entering with a group of friends.

On impulse, he sauntered over for a quiet word.

"Though you'd like to know," he said, drawing Gadsby aside. "Piers is back."

"Piers who?" Gadsby asked without much interest.

Bertie glared at him. "Piers, your cousin by marriage. Piers the bloody viscount. Petteril!"

Gadsby shrugged irritably as though to shake off such unpleasantness. "I know. Maria said something about it. It's upset her mother."

"Not surprised." Bertie allowed himself a moment's amusement before returning to the matter in hand. "Don't think he's been there long." He grinned with considerable contempt. "I went round there earlier to see if it was true his lordship was in residence, and found a back window broken and boarded up. Expect he got in that way. He was always a little runt."

"What, doesn't he have a key for his own house?"

"Only if he knew to go the solicitor, which I doubt he would! Though I suppose the solicitor might have sent it to him. Anyway, point is, he might also let the solicitor close the accounts at Tatts. And Weston's."

"Oh well," Gadsby said. "It was good while it lasted." He paused and a smile curled his lips. "Meet you at Tatt's tomorrow morning if you like—last hurrah?"

Bertie laughed. "Why not?"

Chapter Four

Prowling about the large town house that was now his, Piers tried to shake off both his sense of responsibility for his new stable boy, and his suspicion that with Ape he had bitten off rather more than he could chew. Or wished to chew.

The house was bad enough. Upstairs, on the first floor, was a drawing room, a formal dining room, a morning room and a small library that he might be able to face tomorrow. For today, he decided to abandon them and stay on the ground floor, which held, among other salons, a reception room and a cosy breakfast parlour. He settled in the latter and began to scribble down notes and thoughts.

He heard the sound of the baize door to the servants' quarters swinging shut, but he didn't look up until Ape slouched into the room.

"Whatcher, mister," the boy said amiably. He was wearing the new cap, breeches, shirt and boots, and he wore the jacket unfastened so that it hung loose about his body. A faint flush betrayed his embarrassment. Beneath the cap, the short, untidy hair still needed a comb, but its dirty brown hue had been revealed as a dazzling golden blond.

Piers hid his own uneasiness and sniffed the air. "*A rose by any other name would smell as sweet.* Well done, Ape. No Silver Jug and no dung. What do you want for supper?"

"What you got?" Ape asked, then almost immediately, "What you doing?"

"Making a list of anyone who might have wandered off with the Petteril necklace."

"Well, you can't blame it on servants," Ape said with some satisfaction.

"With the possible exception of my uncle's butler and housekeeper who locked up the house and kept their keys."

"Can you find them?" Ape asked with interest, sitting down beside Piers and appearing to admire his writing.

"Easily, they're with my uncle's widow in Half Moon Street, which makes it extremely unlikely that either of them stole anything. But my aunt certainly has a key. From what you say, so has my cousin Bertie, very probably Maria and Gadsby and even Gussie."

"Who are they?"

"More cousins."

"Why would they steal from you if they're family?"

Because they are entitled, and I, apparently, am not. "They probably don't regard it as stealing," Piers said vaguely, avoiding Ape's young-old eyes. "Besides, my aunt was quite put out not to find the necklace, so presumably it was not she who took it. Or Gussie, for whom she wanted it."

"What you doing with a necklace anyway?"

"It's an heirloom, part of the estate. An antique. Traditionally it is given to the viscount's bride, so it was my aunt's once. Now it is mine to give to my own bride."

Ape stared, in an arrested kind of way. "Who's that, then?"

"Oh, I don't have one. Yet."

"You don't seem to want one," Ape said shrewdly. "In fact, you don't seem to want any of this."

"I don't," Piers admitted. "I like quiet, books, and study. I like teaching, the challenge of making young people who don't care about learning care anyway. I don't like pomp and fuss, or massive responsibility for hundreds of people, or seas of curious faces and interminable conversations about nothing."

He spoke with casual derision and was unnerved to find Ape's shrewd eyes on his face.

"That why you were...drunk last night?"

The faintest hesitation before "drunk" was too telling. Again, Piers dropped his gaze to his hands. "I won't be drunk again," he said briskly, and was surprised to find he meant it—for now at least. "Now, there is—"

"Someone's knocking downstairs," Ape interrupted.

Piers blinked. "You've got ears like a dog's."

"Lord and his like wouldn't knock. Wouldn't come before pitch dark neither."

"Then go and see who it is."

Ape jumped up and ran out the room, back along to the green baize door and down toward the servants' hall. Piers followed more slowly, picking up his cane from the hallstand on the way. But opening the door, he heard only cheerful voices below, then the closing of the door and the sound of Ape trudging back up.

Piers let the door go and hastened back to the breakfast parlour, so that he was sitting down unconcerned when Ape came into the room bearing a large tray and grinning.

"It was a footman from next door. His housekeeper sent him with this because she knows we got no servants yet."

"Bless her heart," Piers said in considerable surprise.

"Maybe it's not so bad to be Lord Nob."

A rare breath of laughter escaped Piers. "Maybe it isn't."

For a while they ate in companionable silence.

Then Ape said, "You can't fence something like your necklace in the normal way. Too easy recognised. A fence'd take the stones out and sell them individually, probably melt down any gold. You'd get nothing like its true worth."

"So, whoever took it is either stupid or desperate," Piers agreed, and popped the final, perfectly cooked and buttered potato into his mouth. He swallowed and sighed. "I shall visit my family tomorrow."

"What will I do?" Ape asked.

"Good question," Piers said.

"It ain't normal for a lord to eat with his stable lad," Ape said, clearly disapproving now that his belly was full.

"That is true. We should have more servants tomorrow. You'll eat in the servants' hall with them."

Ape frowned. "Where will you eat?"

Piers's smile was crooked. "Wherever I like." Except not in an Oxford refectory, not in a quiet inn with a few like-minded scholars or a comfortable sitting room surrounded by books... He blinked. "And you might have more horses to look after."

Ape sat up straighter. "Really?"

"If I find any that I want."

"Cor."

"You can sleep in the kitchen for tonight. I've boarded up the pantry window. Tomorrow it'll be the butler or the housekeeper who decides where you sleep."

Ape nodded happily enough and reached for his pudding. Piers watched with unexpected pleasure. By civilized standards the boy's table manners were disgusting. He held his spoon like a shovel and bent over the bowl, gulping, dribbling and wiping his mouth on the back of his hand. But there was a simple, utter enjoyment in the act of eating that was both funny and touching. Tragic even, but he wouldn't think of that tonight.

"See in the Queen's Head?" Ape said, suddenly lifting his head and catching Piers's gaze.

"I recall it."

"You weren't afraid of Lord and Jakie, were you?"

Piers considered. "No, I don't believe I was."

"Nor the nasty cove in the Silver Jug."

Piers curled his lip. "No."

"That because you're *used* to dealing with scum like them?"

Piers blinked. "No," he admitted.

"You weren't even scared last night!"

"No." Nothing had scared him last night. Except living. He shivered. And saw the admiration in Ape's clear eyes. *Dear God!* "It's not bravery," he said abruptly. "It's..." He floundered.

"Being out of twig?" Ape suggested.

Wearing the wrong clothes. Being in disguise. Piers stared at him. "Actually, yes."

Ape grinned. "And you liked it."

He *had* liked it. Being in disguise as the downtrodden yet slightly dangerous clerk. A role, a play. Like being the viscount instead of the gentle, learned Oxford don. Interesting... Maybe.

After they'd finished eating, Piers returned to the kitchen with Ape and helped him empty the bathwater. After which he showed him the bed nook, left him a lamp, and said good night.

It seemed a bit of a shame that their informal relationship would have to change now, to accommodate their respective positions and the understanding of other servants.

Exhausted, Piers made his way back up to the bedchamber that was traditionally the viscount's. It was a comfortable room, though a little heavy for Pier's taste. It needed lighter colours, less furniture and more books. But it had a fine view over the park—hence the balcony.

Piers swallowed and turned away. Hell, he was the viscount. He could sleep where he liked. Impatiently, he yanked the covers off the bed, piled the pillows on top and dragged them into the room opposite. There, he collapsed on the bed without even lighting a candle, and fell into a deep, blank sleep.

Ape took longer to fall asleep. Used to stone floors and cold, the comfort of a soft mattress, warmth and blankets were not only novelties—like the new night shirt—but oddities. Besides, his mind dwelled constantly on his unexpected new master. He didn't know if Lord Petteril was dicked in the nob to take him on and trust him. Or if Ape was the mad one for being here.

The man bothered him. He was too sad, too alone. Too careless of his safety and his life. Ape wasn't stupid. He knew in his heart as well as his head that the viscount hadn't been drunk last night. He hadn't been going to fall off the balcony. He had been going to jump. And that scared Ape half to death.

What an unforgivable shame to end a life, one that had been given such privilege and kindness, cleverness and courage. Ape didn't understand the man, who was clearly eccentric, even by nob standards, but for some reason, he liked him. He liked the way his eyes sparkled when he thought of problems or saw the funny side of something. At least he wasn't sad *all* the time.

Ape dwelled on the clever, handsome face with the tragic eyes, the swiftness of his movements, especially when striking the threatening Jakie. Ape found he was smiling.

Piers rose early without difficulty. He found a clean shirt and cravat in the viscount's dressing room and realized with some surprise that he was looking forward to the day if not with pleasure, then at least with determination. His mind felt clear and light, even if he knew he was clinging like a drowning man to problems he needed to solve. The necklace. His family. Ape. Servants.

He went down to the kitchen and clattered about for some time with the stove, the kettle, water and cups. He found the remains of bread and butter from last night's meal and munched some standing up, before he yelled for Ape.

There was no answer. Piers walked round to the bed nook, wondering how disappointed he would be to find Ape gone. Actually, it would be simpler. Ape knew too much and had at least one too many secrets of his own. Not that Piers cared.

The mattress was empty, although the blankets had been neatly spread up. The new jacket and spare clothes lay folded on the bed, and the old ones rolled in a ball in the corner.

Ape hadn't *gone*. He'd just stepped out, probably to the stable to see the Professor. Piers went back to making tea, refusing to think about how relieved he was. He didn't want Ape to go back to Lord and crime and the dark, dangerous, filthy-poor world of the Silver Jug and its vile denizens.

A knock at the area door took him along the short passage.

"My name is Jane Bland," said a very superior looking woman in black. She reminded Piers of his Aunt Hortensia, the viscountess. "I have come to be interviewed by Lord Petteril for the position of housekeeper."

"Ah, come in," Piers said amiably. "I'm Petteril. Cup of tea?"

Mrs. Bland was clearly scandalized to be admitted by him and then interviewed by him in the kitchen. They both knew they would not suit, but they went through the motions until, as she departed, she graciously admitted a man and a woman to the kitchen and shook the dust of Petteril House from her sensible shoes.

Mr. and Mrs. Park were a married couple and sought the positions of butler and housekeeper together.

"I know it's not what everyone wants," Park the butler said, "but I assure your lordship we do not bring marital strife to any household."

"Heaven forbid," Piers said, pouring them tea, just as Ape came bursting in through the back door. He wore his new boots and breeches and cap, though his jacket was the old one.

"Cor!" he announced. "I'm starving!"

"I left you some bread and butter. This is Ape," Piers said. "Ape, this is Mr. and Mrs. Park who are considering joining the household."

"He needs looking after," Ape said, sliding into the seat beside Piers. "He's got no food in the house and shouldn't be making his own tea, let alone mine. I looks after his horse."

"I'm sure you do so with great care," Mrs. Park said, "which is probably why it slipped your mind that you are still wearing your cap."

"Eh?" said Ape, pausing to glance from her to Piers, then to Park, and finally caught on. Blushing, he snatched his cap off his head and grinned. "Sorry. He knows I ain't learned good manners yet, but I'm trying. Ain't I, mister?"

Mrs. Park beamed at him, while Piers pretended to read the couple's references. He had already decided they would do.

Piers did not beat about the bush. "The house is not in bad repair, but it has lain neglected for several months. I may want some redecoration in time, but for now it's organization that is required. And a full staff who will answer to you and to me. No one else. The positions are yours if you can face it."

The couple exchanged one short glance. Even so, it was as if they each already knew the other's thoughts. Piers wondered how long they had been married, conscious of a pang that was mostly curiosity. Most marriages that he had observed consisted of *mis*understandings, deliberate and otherwise.

"Thank you, my lord. We gratefully accept," said Park.

"In that case, I'm off to Tattersall's." His gaze landed on Ape, who liked horses. "You might as well come with me, if the Professor is fed and watered?"

"And mucked out again," Ape said cheerfully, springing up from the table and grabbing his cap.

Park seemed to have grasped the boy's background, to some degree at least. "You walk behind his lordship," he told him. "Unless he calls you closer. And address him as my lord, or your lordship, not mister."

"What do I call you?"

"Mr. Park," the butler said sternly. He indicated his wife. "And Mrs. Park."

"They are to be obeyed," Piers added.

"'Course they are," Ape said impatiently. "Can we go now?"

Ape was delighted to be taken with his lordship. He wasn't quite sure yet what he felt about the Parks. They seemed reasonable, for stuffy people, and didn't look at him as if he was something they'd stepped on by accident. On the other hand, Ape was conscious of a pang at the intrusion of anyone else looking after *him*.

Which was stupid. Lords needed lots of people to look after them, and Ape had only been with him part of a day and a night. He had to remember that the viscount could dismiss him as easily as he had taken him on. And probably would, for Ape was hardly a natural servant. He had no idea how to go on, and once his lordship had found his feet, he'd want someone better.

Unless Ape made himself indispensable.

Tattersalls, at Hyde Park Corner, was only a short walk from the house, and turned out to be a horse sale yard. Ape was in heaven. He had never seen so many horses in one place. Ignoring the people gathered there to examine the animals and see them put through their paces, he trailed after Lord Petteril with his mouth open, and all his attention on the horses.

Until, while his lordship was examining some handsome greys, Ape saw the soldier again. Captain Withan. He wasn't wearing uniform today, but an elegant blue coat that fitted perfectly across his broad shoulders, and buff pantaloons that showed off his powerful thighs. He was with a few other men, one of whom nudged him and jerked his head toward Lord Petteril.

"Good God," Captain Withan said, taking what looked like an involuntary step forward. "Petteril?"

His lordship, who had been feeling down the length of a horse's leg, straightened and looked vaguely toward the speaker.

"How do you do?" he said politely and moved on to the next leg.

Captain Withan, however, stuck out his hand in an amused kind of way, forcing his lordship to take it to avoid rudeness. Reluctantly, it seemed, Petteril turned fully toward his cousin and shook hands.

By this time, the man who'd noticed him first was smiling and offering his hand, too. He was about the same age as the captain, equally well-dressed, with a winning smile and twinkling eyes though there were a few deeply etched lines in his face, and a certain slackness that spoke of late nights and too many drinks. Ape had seen such signs in too many much poorer men not to recognize them in this nob.

Dutifully, Petteril shook this man's hand, too, a faint, courteous curve to his lips that could have meant anything, although his sharp eyes did scan both men's faces rapidly.

Ape was confused. Something was wrong in his lordship's manner. It wasn't even dislike—that, Ape could have understood. Certainly, there was discomfort, well-hidden in blandness, but that was only part of it.

He was a bit of a mystery, this gentleman.

"Buying some horse flesh?" the second man asked him cheerfully.

Lord Petteril's gaze barely flickered. They were surrounded by the sights, sounds and smells of horses. "Thought I might."

"Going to cut a dash, Petteril?" the man said amiably, while his eyes mocked.

"Shouldn't think so," his lordship said. "Got your eye on anything in particular?"

"Oh, just looking," Captain Withan said. "You know how it is. Glad to run into you, actually. Came by yesterday, spoke to some ragged urchin who claimed to work for you. He said he'd pass on my message, but I don't suppose he remembered."

The captain hadn't even noticed Ape, who resented being thought brainless, though he supposed ragged was fair enough. Not now, though, in his smart new cap and boots and breeches... He became aware of a subtle change in Lord Petteril.

"Actually, he did tell me. Sorry to miss you. Everything's at sixes and sevens just now."

"Call on me if you need a hand sorting it all out," the dissolute man offered.

"Thank you," Lord Petteril replied politely. "I know where to find you. Excuse me, will you? Got a few things to do today."

"Word to the wise," Captain Withan said, touching his nose. "I wouldn't buy those greys."

Petteril smiled. "Wouldn't you?" he murmured as the two gentlemen wandered off.

Ape crept closer to the viscount. "Who's the other one?"

"Sir Jeremy Gadsby, my cousin Maria's husband." His lordship didn't appear to mind being asked. More than that, for Ape, the confidence of his reply contrasted most oddly with the vagueness of his initial family greetings, and suddenly, he understood why.

Petteril hadn't recognized them.

All sorts of suspicions flew into Ape's head. Were they not his cousins at all? Were they imposters? And if so, why? And why was lordship pretending to know them?

Or was Petteril himself the imposter? Someone who just happened to look like the real viscount?

Chapter Five

Piers bought the greys.

And discovered, when he signed for them, why Cousin Bertie hadn't wanted him to. Apparently, Lord Petteril had bought a few other horses in the last month, including a matched pair for a town carriage, and a large, expensive hunter.

He was thoughtful as he left Tattersalls for the carriage maker's, Ape swaggering along behind him. When Piers had explained the good points about the greys' bodies and movements, the boy had soaked the information up like a sponge. He was clearly thrilled by the prospect of having more horses to look after. Even Piers's warning that he would be hiring an experienced groom whom Ape would also have to obey, did not appear to quench his spirit.

In fact, he was startlingly well behaved while Piers chose a smart, well-sprung curricle. Only as they left again, did Ape burst out, "You going to drive yourself, mister? I mean, my lord."

"I prefer to, when possible."

"Cor."

"In fact, I've been thinking you could be my tiger," he said, probably unwisely.

"Eh?"

"You perch up behind when I'm driving and hold the horses for me when I call in somewhere."

"Me?" Ape squeaked.

"If you prove your skill," Piers said and almost laughed at his own pomposity.

"How do I do that, then?"

"You can walk the Professor up and down the mews, since I won't have time to ride him today."

Ape appeared to be speechless, remembering even to fall behind for the rest of the way home. Here, they walked straight around to the mews, and Piers put the bridle on the horse while Ape watched closely. Piers showed him how to lead the Professor out and walk him without being dragged into a pace he couldn't control. Then it was Ape's turn.

The boy had a light touch, gentle, yet firm when he had to be. And the Professor clearly liked him.

"Can I stay here with him?" Ape asked as Piers picked up his hat to return to the house.

"For now. I might want you to come with me later." He hesitated, but the die seemed to be cast between them. "To my aunt's house. I'd like you to go to her kitchen and listen to the servants. See if you can find out which of them came from here with my aunt, and if any of them have keys, or were instructed to give keys to anyone else."

"To steal the necklace, you mean?"

He shrugged. "Maybe. I doubt any servant would be daft enough, but I need to know. Um...can you be discreet, Ape?" Did he even know what it meant?

Ape grinned. "Like a clam. Mister? I mean, my lord?"

"Yes?" Piers turned back, his mind already on the afternoon.

"How come you didn't know your own cousins?"

Piers had felt it before, the sudden weight of discovery that seemed to crush him. Only this time the weight seemed to bounce off him. Ape already knew worse about him.

"I have an affliction," he announced airily, quite the superior viscount who could do no wrong. "A difficulty in recognizing faces, especially those I don't see often. I have not seen Bertie or Gadsby in five or more years. I only realized who they were when Bertie said he'd spoken to you."

Ape frowned. "But you knew me in the Silver Jug."

Piers allowed himself a crooked smile. "I knew your size and your execrable clothes. Besides, our meeting was somewhat...memorable."

But Ape had already moved on. "That why you don't want to be a lord and have to hobnob with lots of important folk who expect you to know them at once?"

"Yes," he admitted. "Partly."

"Didn't it bother you at the university, too?"

"Not so much. I saw most of the same people every day, and academics are often pretty distracted. Besides, my students seem to expect to keep telling me their names." He clamped his lips together, aware he was saying too much, though Ape looked more intrigued than either pitying or contemptuous.

"So, you don't forget anything else?" he asked. "Just faces?"

"Just faces."

Ape gave a crooked smile. "I got the opposite problem. I can't forget faces I want to. And if they do start to blur, I dream them sharp as ever."

With a surge of pity and helpless anger, Piers guessed they were nightmares. No wonder the smooth, young face had such old, knowing eyes. As if embarrassed, Ape turned away, patting the Professor's neck.

"I'll send for you," Piers said abruptly, and strode away toward the house.

Entering by the back door, he was surprised to see a beautifully dressed young lady elegantly sipping a cup of tea at the kitchen table.

She jumped up at first sight of him, her face splitting into smiles. "Cousin Piers!" she exclaimed, rushing to hug him.

Surprised, he could only pat her shoulder, and guess, "Gussie?"

She gurgled with laughter. "Who else would I be?

She stood back and examined him from head to toe, still beaming. "You're just as I remember you."

"I'm afraid I can't say the same to you." He had a very vague recollection of a lively child, all ringlets and laughter that her mother, clearly, had not managed to curb entirely.

"Just as well, since I was about eleven."

"Um... Why are you in the kitchen? I'm guessing your mother is not with you."

"Lord, no. Your housekeeper—Mrs. Park?—has all the windows open in the public rooms and everyone's cleaning like whirlwinds. She had the scullery maid bring me a cup of tea while I waited for you."

"I have a scullery maid?"

"Apparently, but she's upstairs cleaning right now." The smile died, giving way to a look of apology. "I'm afraid Mama took all your servants to Half Moon Street."

And rather more besides. "She has done me a favour. I prefer to have servants not constantly harking back to the good old days of his late lordship your papa."

"It's good of you to see it that way," she said quietly.

Piers waved her back to the kitchen chair and sat down opposite her. "Your mother tells me you are out this Season. Are you enjoying it?"

"Hugely! There are parties every night, and trips to the theatre and the opera. During the day there are Venetian breakfasts, morning calls, expeditions to the park and the most beautiful shops. Everyone is delightful. I even have a suitor who wants to marry me."

"Goodness. How very grown-up."

She smiled. "Isn't it? And only think, Cousin, you are my guardian."

"I hadn't thought of that. I will have to interview this young man and see if he is good enough for you."

She eyed him with a hint of wariness. "Are you serious?"

He shrugged. "Only if *you* want to marry *him*."

"I haven't made up my mind yet," Gussie said candidly. "Though I do like flirting with him, and Mama approves. I'll introduce him to you at the Amberly ball, if you like."

"Ah," he said, nodding wisely, as he recalled his aunt's words on the subject. "The occasion you are to wear the Petteril necklace. If we can find it."

Gussie laughed. "The Petteril necklace? Lord no, Mama would never let me wear such a thing. She says it's quite unsuitable for a young, unmarried girl."

Piers regarded her. "Does she say so, indeed?"

"Frequently. Because you must know I love rubies. They seem to lend one's cheeks such delightful colour. Here and here." She moved her head, using one finger to trace her shapely cheek bones. "But according to the rules of society, the Petteril necklace is too heavy and regal for me. It's more suited to Mama or even Maria, though Maria doesn't like rubies or garnets. You must marry someone regal to suit them, Piers." She stopped. "I should call you Petteril, now, shouldn't I?"

"I was going to insist on *my lord* at all times."

Her infectious gurgle of laughter broke out again, and he decided he liked this cousin.

"No, you weren't." She set down her cup. "But I should go home before Mama notices I've slipped the leash."

"You didn't come by yourself, did you?" he asked uneasily, knowing Aunt Hortensia would blame him for the transgression.

"Oh, no, I brought my maid, but I left her upstairs to help Mrs. Park. I'll collect her on the way out."

At that moment, Ape all but burst in the kitchen door. "'Here, mister, I mean, my lord, I saw that footman in the mews that brought—" He broke off at the dazzling sight of Gussie, and looked rather wildly at Piers for a clue as to what he should do.

"My stable lad, Ape," Piers told Gussie. "Ape, you may bow to my cousin, Miss Gussie, and wait for me."

Ape jerked a very speedy bow and spoiled any effect of subservience by a cheeky grin. Gussie, looking both surprised and amused, grinned back.

Piers took his cousin by the arm, walked upstairs with her, and opened the baize door onto a positive hive of activity. Young men on ladders were cleaning windows and chandeliers. All the public room doors and shutters were open to admit light and breeze and the chatter of maids.

Park materialized from one of the rooms. "Good afternoon, my lord. May I assure your lordship that guests will not be shown to the kitchen again?"

"I think your assurance has disappointed Miss Withan."

Gussie smiled. "Only because kitchens remind me of home, and Cookie saving us extra cake." She raised her voice to call, "Are you there, Smithy? We're going home. Goodbye, Park! Goodbye, *my lord*!" She swept across the hall and Park was only just in time to open the front door for her. A breathless maid ran out of the room on the right and scurried out on her heels.

Park closed the door. "Some garments have been delivered from Weston, my lord. I took the liberty of placing them in the master bedroom. I have been searching for a suitable valet for your lordship, but no doubt you will prefer to interview them yourself."

Piers almost groaned. What the devil did he want with a valet? Some Friday-faced, superior being, always there in his way, assisting as if he were a child who could neither dress himself nor find his own things. He supposed it was necessary to his new status, but it was an affectation he could live more happily without.

"No doubt," Park added, "you will have your own ideas of the duties you will wish your valet to perform. And not perform."

Piers, about to trudge up the stairs, paused to cast Park a thoughtful glance. He allowed the smile to flicker on his lips, then climbed the stairs with a lighter tread. It was true a body servant could be useful, looking after his clothes and keeping his rooms tidy. Even pulling off his boots. Such a man might even be an extra obstacle to stepping back out onto the balcony. But Park was right. Piers was the master.

"Cor," Ape said an hour or so later, when Lord Petteril came to extract him from the stable.

His lordship looked remarkably fine in morning attire made to fit him perfectly. His tall, lean frame seemed somehow *elegant* now, rather than flung together and held loosely in a haphazard collection of comfortable old clothes. Even his chestnut hair, too long for fashion, looked more refined than tangled. His cravat was starched rather than crumpled and set in place with a plain gold pin. His only ornaments were a fob watch and not one, but two quizzing glasses hung by black ribbons around his neck.

Ape, struck temporarily dumb by the far from unattractive vision before him, wished heartily for the return of the awkward yet easy-going gentleman of the morning. Yet he couldn't take his eyes off the handsome lord of the present. He contented himself with staring at the quizzing glasses, which appeared to unnerve his lordship.

"Too much?" he inquired.

Ape shook his head. "Why two?" he managed.

"One for reading, if I need to. Saves remembering the spectacles which I tend to leave in various places anyway. The other is for more distant observations. It was a fancy that took me this morning, since I am inventing his lordship as I go."

Silly relief flooded Ape. He was still the same man. "I like his lordship."

"Then shut the Professor in and follow me around to Half Moon Street."

Fifteen minutes later, mindful of his instructions, Ape sat in the Dowager Lady Petteril's kitchen which, he was glad to observe, was smaller than his lordship's, although the cook was pleasant and shoved a cup of tea and a slice of cake in his direction.

"So, what do you for his lordship, then?" she asked, sitting down comfortably and wiping her hands on her apron.

"I'm to be his tiger, and stable lad. And," Ape added, sticking with the story he and his lordship had concocted, "not knowing this bit of London, I'm just following him around so I can be more useful later."

"Ain't he got any other servants?" asked a footman in livery. His expression was one of curiosity mixed with a hint of guilt.

"Oh, yes, and more all the time. Didn't you all used to work there?"

"Moved with her ladyship to be sure of the position," the footman replied.

"Hold your tongue, Horace," the cook said, clearly annoyed. "No one knew his lordship's plans, so we were glad of the choice her ladyship gave us."

"Miss the big house," sighed a passing maid. "Although to be sure a position with a man of no consequence would have been a step down."

Ape bridled. "No consequence? What d'you mean by that? He's the viscount!"

The maid looked down her nose at him. "Only by the misfortune of his brother and cousins all dying within a year of each other. And his father and his uncle. No one ever pretended he was a *suitable* viscount. Lets the whole family down."

Ape curled his lip. "That what your ladyship tells you? Or your butler?"

"Hold your tongue, Nora," the cook snapped.

"Why?" Ape demanded. "I want to know why you got no respect for his lordship."

"Of course, we respect his lordship!" Cook said in sudden alarm. "So don't go telling him any different. Nora's got no call to call him unsuitable because obviously he is so suitable. Some of us just remember him from the old days, when they were all boys together. Master

George, who should have inherited the title, and his younger brother, Master John, who died in Portugal, God rest him. Their cousins, Ivor and your Mr. Piers used to be with them a lot. He were bookish, tended to sickness, not a big, lively lad like the others, and they made fun of him for it. He weren't great at standing up for himself."

Ape read between the lines with perfect understanding and not a little disgust. "They bullied him 'cause he was younger. Don't see how that makes him unsuitable."

"It doesn't, of course," Cook said hastily, glaring at Nora, who sniffed and subsided. "The family's just grieving and coming to terms with the changes."

And his lordship *wasn't* grieving? Weren't they his family, too? His father and his brother were among the dead listed by Nora. Ape kept his gaze on the housekeeper, trying to hide his anger.

She pursed her lips. "Some of us takes their part too closely, sympathizes aloud where we should know better. Poor gentleman couldn't help the death of his brother and his cousins any more than her ladyship could."

Ape, remembering his instructions, swallowed the remains of his indignation. "Natural, though. Loyalty," he allowed, so they'd think he wouldn't tell Lord Petteril, and then switched tack suddenly enough, he hoped, to catch them off guard. "Who's got the old keys, then?"

"What old keys?" the cook asked, bewildered.

"For Petteril House. You shouldn't be going in and out of there if you ain't working for him. You made your own beds and should lie in them."

"And that's enough of your cheek, my lad," the cook said in apparent outrage. "No servant here would *dare* go back there. Got no reason to, neither. So, you keep a civil tongue in your head in my kitchen."

Horace the young footman, munching his slice of cake, added, "You got it wrong, anyway, lad. Mrs. Roberts and Mr. Herries might have taken the keys for safety when we all left, but they gave them to the family, not servants. I know, because I saw them in the front hall."

"What, the keys? Or the family? All together?" Ape said with blatant disbelief.

Horace coloured and tried to look down his nose. "No, 'course not. But Mr. Herries gave his set to Captain Withan."

Did he now? Interesting. "Who'd your housekeeper give hers to, then?"

"I don't know," the footman admitted.

"And shouldn't be gossiping about it neither," the cook said severely. "If Mr. Herries catches you, you'll be dismissed without a character, and quite right, too. Now, Ape, how long does his lordship mean to remain in London?"

The question gave Ape a nasty moment. He'd never even thought of Lord Petteril leaving town. But all these nobs had big country estates. It was where their money came from, and his lordship did not care to mix with crowds of people whose faces all looked the same to him. Ape could understand that, but not the sudden panic in his own breast at the thought of being alone again.

He needed to get a grip and make alternative plans.

Chapter Six

Rather to his own surprise, Piers enjoyed the expressions of those gaping at him in his aunt's drawing room. Although the butler, Herries, had announced him, everyone looked satisfyingly stunned.

Aunt Hortensia sprang to her feet in astonishment and then appeared annoyed with herself, as though she had not planned to rise to greet him.

"Piers," she said sharply. "What a pleasant surprise."

Piers bowed. The elegance seemed to come with his new clothes, like the violence in yesterday's clerk. *Clothes maketh the man...*

Gussie—easily spotted because she was wearing the same dress as when he had seen her an hour or so ago—was all but crowing with delight. "Now I see!" she exclaimed, clapping her hands. She curtseyed deeply. "*My lord.* So, what do you think? Has Maria changed as much as me?"

Thankfully, there was only one other lady in the room, a handsome young woman almost as amazed as her mother. She had the same glossy, chestnut locks as Gussie, but straighter. More refined. There seemed to be nothing of the child left in Maria. Even her blatant astonishment was quickly hidden in a bland, social smile.

What had they been expecting? With a twinge of shame, Piers recalled his meeting with his aunt yesterday, among the edges of the blackness. He must have seemed vague to the point of imbecilic. Though, seriously, did they imagine the university would have honoured him as it had, were he simply a fool with a viscount for an uncle?

"Cousin Piers," Maria said faintly. "I doubt I have changed, but you certainly have."

"Not in the least. It's only a new coat."

"Cutting a dash after all?" grinned the only other gentleman present. He looked rather like Jeremy Gadsby, whom he had encountered at Tattersalls this morning.

"You remember Maria's husband, Sir Jeremy," Hortensia said. She was still treating him as an idiot, and in this case he was grateful.

"Of course," Piers murmured. "We met this morning."

"You didn't buy the greys, did you?" Gadsby asked, a hint of unease in his easy smile.

Piers smiled back. "In fact, I did. Most enlightening."

Briefly, Gadsby's unease flared into alarm.

Piers made the most of it. "The hunter or the matched bays?" he inquired.

Gadsby understood at once that he'd been rumbled. He didn't even blush, though his gaze did fall away. "The bays," he muttered. "Naturally, I shall pay you back."

"Naturally," Piers said gently.

Maria and her mother were exchanging bewildered glances. Gussie frowned, raising her eyebrows to Piers for an explanation which he had no intention of giving. Yet.

"Ring for tea, Augusta," Hortensia said, and Gussie obeyed.

"I'm very glad to have caught you at home," Piers said, seating himself when the ladies had done so. "I wanted to say, aunt, you need not worry about collecting the keys we talked about yesterday." He frowned in an effort of remembrance. "Or if we didn't talk about them, we should have. In any case, the locks are changed."

Gadsby turned his head hastily to the window. Piers suspected it was to hide guilt or shame, though of what he could hardly tell.

"Really, Piers, is that not unnecessarily vulgar?" Hortensia snapped. "Anyone would think you do not trust your family!"

I don't. He raised one eyebrow. "On the contrary. Anyone would think I had closed the stable door after the horse has bolted. The Petteril necklace is still gone."

Hortensia's colour heightened in clear outrage. "You cannot imagine the thief used our keys!"

"It is the obvious conclusion, since the thief knew exactly where and how to find the necklace."

"Yes, but the house was broken into, old boy," Gadsby said patiently. "Bertie told us one of your back windows had been broken and boarded up."

"True, but the necklace was already gone by then. And seriously, what self-respecting burglar would take the rubies and leave the pearls?"

Everyone stared at him. He could almost see their minds working, puzzling, suspecting, discarding. Only Hortensia drew herself up to her full height. "Are you accusing one of us? You dare to cast such vile aspersions in my own home?"

Piers held his expression to one of mild surprise. "I said only that the thief used a house key."

"Well, you have one of those too, old boy," Gadsby pointed out into the silence.

Ah, direct attack. Piers turned to regard him.

Hortensia said, "Exactly!" with an air of triumph.

So, they would close ranks and turn on him, even now. It crossed his mind to simply walk out and leave them to stew, never see any of them again. After all, it's what he had effectively done by losing himself in Oxford. He felt a fierce tug of longing for the old life.

But only for an instant. The intellectual problem of the necklace was still there. Gussie was looking appalled and anxious. His entire family was behaving like naughty children, and he had all the responsibilities of the viscountcy. Bizarrely, it seemed he was the only adult.

"Mr. Devon, your ladyship," Herries said from the door, and Hortensia, instantly distracted, cast a delighted look at Gussie, who blushed.

Mr. Devon was a handsome, fashionable young man with short, fair hair and an easy smile. Gussie's suitor, Piers apprehended, and favoured, judging by her mother's gracious welcome and the fact that she waved him to the seat beside Gussie on the sofa.

"Oh, and you won't know my nephew, newly arrived in town," she added, as Devon's gaze landed on Piers in passing. For a moment, it seemed she could not actually get the words over her lips, then she said in a rush. "Lord Petteril."

If Hortensia was blind as to whose consent was necessary for Gussie's marriage, Devon clearly was not. His eyes widened slightly, as though surprised, then he bowed.

"Very happy to meet you, my lord. I have heard so much about you,"

Piers smiled. "I'm sure you have."

Devon sat beside Gussie, just as tea arrived, and the general, pointless conversation sprang up, about the weather, who was attending what party, and the doings of people Piers had never heard of. He occupied himself watching Gussie flirt elegantly with Devon, and examining the faces of Maria, Gadsby and Hortensia, none of whom paid him any attention, apart from providing him with a cup of tea and a scone. It struck him, almost with surprise, that none of them were very happy, except for Gussie.

Maria, speaking little more than platitudes, made small, restless little movements with her feet and hands, and her eyes were vaguely discontented. Sir Jeremy Gadsby, her husband, behaved like any fashionable man, too sophisticated to be excited by anything they spoke about. And yet behind the bored lines of his face, Piers read a kind of hunger. Had that always been there? He couldn't remember. The last time he had seen Gadsby, Piers had been more interested in escape. Was that how Gadsby felt now?

Well, who wouldn't want to escape the Withans?

Devon, apparently, who was inviting Gussie to drive with him in the park, remembering to ask permission of her mother, who smiled benignly as she granted it.

Piers decided to make conversation with Maria.

"He seems a pleasant fellow," he said, startling her though he spoke quietly.

She blinked rapidly, following his gaze. "Henry Devon? Oh yes. He's Sindon's heir, you know."

"Sindon?"

"Lord Sindon. He has land in the north I believe. It would be an excellent match for Augusta. And quite a feather in her cap to fix his interest so early in the Season."

"Has she?" Piers asked, startled.

"Well, of course he has not offered for her yet, but he does seem smitten, don't you think?"

"I'm no judge," Piers said frankly. "Do you like him?"

"He is all that is amiable, and quite unexceptionable."

Which was hardly the same, though he wasn't sure Maria realized it. "Gussie appears to like him."

For the first time a genuine smile touched Maria's lips. "Gussie is enjoying herself. The whole Season is one long ball for her."

"Then Devon is merely one of many admirers?"

"Yes," Maria allowed. "But he is the most persistent."

And the most favoured, clearly, at least by her family. Devon, in the midst of his conversation with Gussie, glanced up and caught Piers watching him. Instantly, his lips quirked into a smile.

Too eager to please. Well, one would be, Piers supposed, if one wanted permission to marry a fellow's ward. More responsibility. With a sigh, he rose. "Forgive me, aunt, I must take my leave. Much to do."

"I can imagine," Hortensia said. "I wish you would let me help with finding suitable servants. It cannot be pleasant rattling about loose in that great house with no one to do anything."

"Oh, it's full of people, now," Piers assured her.

"What, one urchin you've persuaded to look after your horse?" Gadsby said in amusement. Clearly, Bertie had mentioned his encounter with Ape. Or perhaps Gussie had. "He's probably stealing from you as we speak."

"Oh, Ape's not stealing from me," he said, leaving only a very subtle emphasis on *Ape*. "Good afternoon, all. Thank you for tea, aunt." He bowed and sauntered out. Everyone murmured a farewell, though only Gussie's and Devon's sounded very friendly.

"Learn anything?" Piers murmured as Ape trotted along at his heels.

"The butler gave his set of keys to your cousin, Captain Withan. What did you learn?"

Piers sighed. There was so much petty guilt in his family, it was hard to distinguish it from anything more important. "None of them seem worried about the necklace. I could almost imagine it's an invented stick to beat me with. My aunt claimed she wanted it for my cousin Gussie to wear, but Gussie says she's never allowed to wear it because her mother believes it is unsuitable for young girls."

"Maybe she wants it for herself and doesn't think you'd ever be around to see her wear it."

"But would she risk me involving magistrates and the law? And gossip below stairs?"

"None of them mentioned the necklace," Ape said.

"Did they talk about the family?"

"Defensive of them."

"Anything about my cousin Gussie and her apparent suitor? Fellow called Devon?"

Ape shook his head. "They wondered whether you were staying in London, though. Maybe some of them wants their old jobs back."

"No chance."

Ape grinned, though the amusement seemed to vanish quicker than usual. "*Are* you staying, though?"

"For a week or so at least. I'll need to go to Wiltshire soon, however. Ape, who would know if this wretched necklace was being fenced?"

"You don't want to know that."

"No, I probably don't. Hypothetically... that is if you had to, could you find out if the rubies are, as it were, in circulation? Anywhere in London?"

"Sure."

Piers blinked at him. The offer was immediate, and it didn't sound like a boast. On the other hand, Ape's face looked suddenly paler than usual. Which confirmed more than one of his suspicions. "Tatty at the Silver Jug, then."

"I didn't say that!" Ape said in sudden panic.

"No, I'm guessing," Piers said apologetically. "And it doesn't actually matter, because I'm pretty sure the necklace *isn't* being fenced. And on the subject of Tatty, I don't want you going back to St. Giles at all."

For an instant, he thought he saw a blaze of hope in the look the boy flung at him, and then he just looked cheeky again.

"Can't stop me, though, can you, mister?"

"Not in your free time. And I haven't given you any of that, yet have I?"

"No, nor any pay." Honesty seemed to compel him to add, "Though I've had a powerful lot of food."

Piers regarded him thoughtfully. He'd grown quickly used to Ape, but there were hundreds—thousands—of children like him in the slums and back streets only yards from the gracious street they walked in now.

"Did you ever go to school, Ape?"

"Don't be daft."

"Can you read?"

Ape cast him an eloquent look.

"Would you like to?"

"I'd like a lot of things."

"I'll teach you."

Ape's jaw dropped. A tangled array of expressions flashed across his face, far too fast to read. "Why?" he blurted.

"It's useful." A sudden surge of something very like peace filled him. "For everyone. I believe you've just given me an excellent idea."

"I have?"

"I'll make arrangements."

Passing the end of his own mews at the side of Chapel Street, he turned up, and Ape followed, unusually silent. Until they caught sight of Park and a smart curricle and two perfectly matched grey horses.

Uttering a squeal, Ape dashed past Piers and ran toward the new arrivals. Piers found he was grinning.

Naturally, the new horses and curricle had to be tried out. Benson, the new groom who appeared to have materialized, harnessed the horses with quiet efficiency, and Ape was taught where to perch and hang on at the back.

Piers climbed into the carriage and took up the reins. "Let them go!"

As he had suspected, the greys were full of energy, strong and perfectly matched. They were a little too eager, at first, but Piers held them steady and in no time, they were high stepping their way toward Hyde Park with perfect obedience.

Judging by the happy exclamations that occasionally burst out from the back of the vehicle, Ape too was enjoying the ride, and that made Piers grin. It was a lovely spring afternoon, the sun pleasantly warm, the breeze bracingly cool. New leaves were bursting out on the trees, and daffodils swayed brightly along the paths.

It came to Piers that he was happy.

A small moment, as bursts of happiness generally were, but one to be treasured and remembered. Especially when the park suddenly filled up with other fashionable carriages, a few driven by smart ladies, and he realized he had mistimed his jaunt to coincide with the fashionable hour for promenading in the park. Gentlemen on horseback and young ladies walking with chaperones filled the paths, preventing the quick escape that was his instinctive response.

Instead, he remembered that he was twigged out as the viscount. He adopted a suitably aloof expression, touched his whip to his hat when passing ladies, and spoke to no one as he made for the nearest gate.

Until Ape said, "Look, mister, that's your cousin."

"Which one?" Piers asked. "And where?"

"Miss Gussie. Coming toward you, just behind the black horse—in the phaeton with the pretty, blond nob."

Piers recalled that Gussie had in fact made an arrangement to drive with Mr. Henry Devon. Yes, that looked like Gussie, and the man with her *could* be Devon... Abruptly, the inevitable anxiety he was hiding vanished in reality, for Gussie, at this moment, was *not* happy.

Had he ever seen her unhappy before? A child's brief cry for a skinned knee, a temper tantrum at the treatment of her older brothers and cousins—storms quickly vented before the sunshine of her nature prevailed. Now, there were no tears, but there was something too rigid in her straight, ladylike posture. Her gloved hands were gripped together in her lap, quite unmoving, and though her face was composed into a pleasant smile, it was too fixed. Her companion was speaking quite happily, apparently unaware of her distress. Only when she shook her head did he glance at her in surprise. And then she saw Piers.

Abruptly her smile was real, and with more than a hint of relief. "Cousin Piers! Oh, pull up, Mr. Devon. Piers, what beautiful horses."

"Thank you, Gussie, so I think." The carriages halted, facing each other. "Mr. Devon."

"My lord." Devon looked over the horses with an approving eye. "Very fine."

"I believe so. Just trying them out."

"Oh, might I have a try at the ribbons?" Gussie asked eagerly.

"No, but I'll take you a turn around the park if you wish."

"Oh, I do!"

"But Lady Petteril expects me to bring you home," Devon protested.

"I shall meet you at the gate in five minutes," Gussie said, already beginning to climb down, so that Devon was too slow to help her.

Not so Ape, who suddenly scrambled down to help her into the curricle beside Piers. Clearly, he had been paying attention and absorbing the behaviour of others in the park. Piers was both impressed and amused.

Gussie bestowed a smile on Ape, who grinned back before bolting back up to his perch. Devon looked slightly disconsolate, though he maintained his smile as Piers saluted him casually with his whip. Gussie didn't pay him any attention at all.

Piers urged his horses on again along the drive without looking at her. "Quarrelled?"

"Sort of," Gussie admitted. "Perhaps he is not as amusing as I thought. Not all the time at any rate."

"Who is?"

"True." She said no more, seemingly lost in her own thoughts.

"Do you want to tell me?" he asked.

She shook her head. "Not yet."

"Shall I have a word and send him about his business?" This time, he glanced at her, and she bestowed a genuine, beaming smile upon him.

"Not yet," she said again. "But I'm very glad to see you."

It was slightly more than five minutes before Piers met Devon at the gate. Ape, with remarkable efficiency, handed Gussie down from the curricle and helped her up into Devon's phaeton in front.

"After you," Piers said amiably to Devon, and there was nothing for Devon to do but drive out of the park and set off for Half Moon Street.

Chapter Seven

By the time they returned to Petteril House, Piers began to feel he was juggling all too many duties and responsibilities. Much as he had done at Oxford with his own studies, the needs of his various students, and instructions from his professors. But here, he had opportunities to delegate.

Instead of gathering the entire new staff together and making a pompous announcement, he had a quick word with the Parks.

"Will you inform the staff that I will be available each morning between nine and ten of the clock to teach reading and writing to those who cannot? It is not compulsory, but those who wish to learn should come to the library."

Their eyes widened, mirroring each other.

"Including female staff?" Mrs. Park asked.

"*All* staff, inside and outside. Be sure they understand it is not a test, merely a...gratuity. It will make no difference to their employment here whether or not they attend. Though those merely wishing to avoid their duties will be quickly spotted and sent back to them."

"Thank you, my lord," Mr. Park said, bewildered but impressed.

"Is your lordship happy with the staff we have engaged so far?" Mrs. Park asked.

"I'm sure I will be."

"Mrs. Gale, the cook is quite a lucky find. She is looking forward to showing you her skills at dinner."

Piers glanced at his watch. "I have to go out now, but I shall be back to dine at eight."

Which did not give him a great deal of time. But at least he did not yet have a valet to dodge. He felt a certain amount of glee, like a child dressing up, as he changed his smart new clothes for those of the "dangerous clerk", with ink-stained cuffs, old hat and trusty cane. And the reading glasses through which the world was a little hazy. He stuffed them in his pocket for later.

He swung a traveling cloak about him to hide his garb and held the old hat inside his cloak. Then he ran downstairs, nodded to the footman who opened the door for him and walked quickly toward Oxford Street.

He caught a cab to the edges of St. Giles and paid it off. Then, with a quick, uneasy glance at the sky—he really did not want to be here after dark—he plunged into the narrower streets toward the Silver Jug. Inevitably, he took a couple of wrong turnings, but he had learned from Ape and avoided anything that looked like a blind alley. A washerwoman weighed down by her load, put him back on the right track again, and with remarkable speed he found himself back in the Silver Jug.

The tavern was busier and even smellier than when he was last here. A stray dog loped about, no doubt looking for Ape to feed it scraps. A few of the denizens were drinking and laughing, but most looked furtive, watchful, and as if they'd knife you as soon as look you in the eye.

In character, Piers walked straight up to the counter, glancing around him only enough to appear sensible rather than afraid. Two men stood behind the bar, serving mostly ale, but also gin, and rum. One was young, scarred down the right side of his face. Piers ignored him and fixed the older man with a friendly eye.

"Good evening to you," he said amiably in the clerk's accent of one trying to sound better than he was. "I'm looking for one Tatty."

"Don't know any Tatty," came the surly response.

"That's unfortunate. I was told he could help with my ruby problem."

"What sort of problem does the likes of you have with rubies?"

"Lack of them," Piers replied with a beaming smile. "Where should I go to look?"

"I serve ale, not jewels."

"Then I'll have a pint of your ale and I hope it's better than the last time I was in here."

"You've never been in here," Tatty scoffed.

"Beg to differ. Spoke to a young fellow called Ape and had cause to teach some manners to a snivelling gent who couldn't keep his hands to hisself."

Tatty's eyes met his at last. "That was you, was it? Where's Ape? He don't get paid if he ain't here."

"I pay him now."

Tatty shrugged. "Well watch him, or he'll bleed you. In more ways than one."

"Oh, we understand each other pretty well," Piers said significantly. "Which is why I know who to ask about rubies for sale."

Tatty, who had been pouring his ale, moved to a quieter space on the counter to set it down.

Piers followed and closed his fingers around the grubby handle. "Not just any rubies. These would have come up in the last week."

"Been nothing in months," Tatty said.

"I don't just mean around here," Piers clarified. "I mean anywhere in London. Would you hear that kind of thing?"

Tatty cast him a look of scorn. "I know my own trade, which means I know the competition all over. Do you a nice garnet today, if you want, and I know a man with a topaz set, all nice and new, but no rubies. Not anywhere. You got wrong information." He seemed rather pleased by that. "Hope you didn't get it from Ape."

"No, just where to ask. And truth to tell, it's the answer I expected. But one likes to know."

"Does one?" Tatty mocked. "Does one know to look out for Lord?"

Piers considered him. "One knows that if Lord—or anyone else—comes after Ape, the law will be all over the Queen's Head like the worst rash you ever saw. I got friends who can do that. Pretty sure he'd hang. Otherwise, I got no interest in him. Or you."

Piers put down a generous coin and walked jauntily out of the door.

Outside, dusk was falling, and the dingy, unwelcoming alleys had grown positively threatening. A couple of youths stepped out of a doorway in front of him. Piers smiled fiercely and twirled his cane, and they melted back into the gloom.

He didn't make the mistake of rejoicing. He kept moving, quick, steady and watchful until, with huge relief, he reached the broader, busier streets he knew and a hackney to take him home.

From the area steps, Ape saw Lord Petteril leave the house and walk away. He wore a cloak and no hat, though as Ape climbed the steps, he saw the cloak billow and then a hat was clapped on his head. But still, Ape knew his lordship was out of twig. Something in the way he moved gave it away quite clearly. His lordship was up to something, and Ape regarded it as his job to look after him.

Ape was in the street before his thought was finished, already following Petteril before he realized he had not thought it through. He was meant to ask permission before he left—of Benson at the very least, if not Mr. Park. It was also possible his lordship did not want Ape's company or his oversight. What if he was going to see some woman? Or women? If they weren't respectable, he might well prefer to go in disguise.

Ape slowed up, scowling. He didn't like to think of Petteril in such company but he knew perfectly well these things were part of life. His lordship hadn't asked for Ape to accompany him and after his first instinct to protect—which was silly, in any case—Ape was loathe to interfere where he was neither required nor wanted. He had no reason to imagine Lord Petteril needed help.

Reluctantly, Ape turned back toward the house. But, hell's bells, he was out now, and freedom called. Grinning, Ape took off with a massive sense of relief. Being respectable was all very well—put food in your belly and kept you warm, and he couldn't deny it was interesting here—but, Gawd, he was *trapped* in the small space between the servants' hall and the mews, and he was far too used to going where he pleased.

Also, he decided, if he was about his lordship's business, then he was doing nothing wrong. And the best he could do for him was to find this necklace. One of his stuck-up family had prigged it. And quite beside the outrage, Lord Petteril needed to know who, for his own peace. It wasn't as if he could just run away, like Ape. And his family *wouldn't* run because they were sponging off him.

Hands in pockets, Ape found his way back to Half Moon Street, where the old Lady Petteril lived with Miss Gussie. If he wandered into the kitchen with some excuse, just when the family was being served and everyone was busy, he could probably slip past and into the main part of the house where he could search.

He went cold inside at the thought of getting caught there. Would Lord Petteril understand what he was doing, or would he think Ape had gone back to cracking and prigging?

Before he could swing down the area steps to the servants' entrance, someone in a bright red coat sailed out of the front door and swaggered off up the street.

Captain Withan.

In the captain, Ape recognized someone profoundly dishonest, not just with other people but with himself. Withan did what he liked because he told himself he was entitled to. And to Ape, the captain was a far likelier thief than the old woman or Gussie.

Accordingly, he changed his plan and slouched after Captain Withan into the teeming chaos of Piccadilly, where he almost lost him in the crowds of carriages and carts, pedestrians and barrow sellers. But then he caught sight of the brave red coat whisking up St. James Street and hastily jumped over an empty barrow as he bolted after his quarry.

A few more turns, and the captain entered a house using a key. Ape couldn't believe his luck. Withan had gone home. So, all Ape needed to do was wait until he went out again and search the ken.

While he waited, he snooped. This wasn't a big home like Petteril House or even the old lady's place in Half Moon Street. It was a lodging house. Captain Withan and another young man rented rooms here, though it was nothing like the lodging houses Ape had seen in St. Giles with a whole family—or more—crammed into a single shabby room.

At one point, lounging around the front of the house, he fell into conversation with the valet who worked for the tenant who was not Captain Withan, an amiable young man, apparently, currently getting drunk with his friends before a disreputable night on the town.

Ape, who hadn't actually thought of Bertie having a servant himself, said uneasily, "Just you and him here then?"

"No, we've just got the rooms at the top. Military man has the rooms on the first floor."

"Is his servant military too?" Ape asked, as though making a joke.

"He seems to do for himself. Rumour says his family keeps him short. Though I've seen him on some damned fine horses, and my master says his wine is always the best."

Ape breathed a sigh of relief and wandered off.

It was dark by the time Ape slipped in the back door while a kitchen maid was putting out some rubbish. Fortunately, the lamps were lit, and there were plenty nooks and crannies in which to hide. An older man wandered past, almost brushing his coat tails against Ape. Several young men, clearly the worse for drink, clattered down the stairs from the top floor and vanished into the street in a cloud of laughter and loud voices. But it began to seem as if Petteril's Cousin Bertie was staying in for the evening.

Ape wondered if he should go home.

And then, without warning, the captain came out of a door on the first floor, locked it and sauntered downstairs and out the front door. Immediately, Ape sprang up.

On their first encounter, Ape had told Lord Petteril he wasn't on the dub lay—picking locks—but this hadn't always been true. He'd learned to deal with most locks before he even came to St. Giles, and he still had his spiky little tools in the pocket of the baggy old jacket he still preferred to the new, closer-fitting one.

It was the work of a bare minute—his skill had grown rusty—to get into Bertie's rooms, light the nearest lamp and shut the door.

Bertie's lodgings consisted of a sitting room and a bedchamber, both kept clean and mostly tidy. Ape wasted no time but searched his way through every drawer and cupboard. He found a few tie pins and sleeve buttons, a couple of rings, mountains of bills and notes of gaming debts, but no necklace. Not even under the mattress.

Annoyed and frustrated, Ape turned out the lamp and departed, remembering to turn he lock in place behind him. So, Bertie didn't have the necklace in his rooms. Didn't mean he hadn't stolen it in the first place. He'd probably pawned it or sold it already. That's what Lord Petteril clearly thought, judging by the questions he'd asked earlier about fences and Tatty.

Frustrating though. Ape had rather hoped to swagger home with the necklace in his pocket and present it to his lordship with triumph. He had the feeling there would be little surprise that Bertie was the culprit.

A man's annoyed voice came from the direction of the kitchen, scolding relentlessly. There would be no quick escape in that direction. Ape crept to the front door, opened it and bolted into the night.

A hand clamped over his shoulder. "What were you doing in there, boy?" a man growled. Worse, Ape glimpsed the red sleeve in the glow of the nearest lamp and recognized the voice at Captain Withan's. And his grip was bruisingly strong.

However, Ape had lived on the streets for years, dodging the law and villains and angry citizens alike. He dipped, wriggled and bolted with a combination of speed and force that took the captain completely by surprise.

He leapt up behind a passing hackney, clinging on and keeping his face averted from the captain, who shouted after him, but didn't seem to be pursuing. In any case, Ape jumped off in Piccadilly and lost himself in the crowd before he skirted the park Green Park and set off for home.

Maria, Lady Gadsby, had dismissed her maid and climbed into bed although she had not yet blown out the last candle when she heard the sound of her husband entering the dressing room between their bedchambers. She sat up, her heart beating faster, praying he would come in.

His hand touched the door, hesitating, then, perhaps seeing the faint glimmer of the candle, he opened it and came in.

"Ah, you are awake," he said awkwardly.

When had such unease entered their relationship? When he realized Maria had married him for love? When she had failed to produce any children? Or when money had become a worry?

"Yes, I am not long in. Did you have a pleasant evening?"

"Oh, much as usual, you know."

So, he had lost again. Her heart ached for him, for he was trapped in that spiral where winning was the only way out. And one could not win if one did not play.

She took his hand and drew him gently down to sit on the bed. "One can't win every day. What did you think of my cousin Piers?"

"Petteril?" Surprised by the question, Jeremy considered. "He was a bit insulting about the necklace and changing the locks, but I probably would be, too, in his place. Certainly, he's not the slow top Bertie and your mother make him out to be."

Maria waved one dismissive hand. "Bertie's an ass."

Jeremy laughed, lightening his face back into the boyish good looks she recalled from their wedding five years ago. She smiled in relief, but his mirth died as quickly as it had sprung up. "Am I an ass, too?" he asked ruefully.

"Of course not," she whispered, reaching up to stroke his hair.

He caught her hand but bent to kiss her. Then he kissed her again and they fell slowly back against the pillows.

Chapter Eight

Piers woke naturally with the first light of day, and fifteen minutes later, dressed in new riding clothes, strode around to the mews. He was rather pleased when not only the Professor but the new greys acknowledged his presence. He gave them all carrots purloined from the kitchen, where the new cook, Mrs. Gale, was already up and preparing breakfast.

Benson, the groom was up too, stretching and yawning, and inside he found Ape munching on an apple, though he bounced to his feet hopefully as soon as he saw Piers.

"Are you driving again, mister? My lord?" he asked eagerly.

"No, not yet. Benson, I need the Professor saddled. Ape, you watch him and learn. You can practise later."

In fact, Ape helped with the bridle, while watching Benson place the saddle and fasten girths.

"Did you manage to make yourself comfortable up there?" Piers asked Benson, jerking his head to the room above the stable.

"Very, sir. The boy slept up there, too."

Piers paused, very briefly, in the act of swinging himself in the saddle. Here was a juggling ball he had dropped and would have to deal with very soon. Which was a pity. He rather liked things as they were, and he was sure Ape did, too.

He only nodded and set off toward Hyde Park. He found the park quiet at this time of day, though not deserted. A couple of like-minded souls nodded to him as they cantered past. He nodded back, although he knew he wouldn't recognize them if he met them again. It didn't matter. Lord Petteril wasn't obliged to recognize anyone, only give everyone the minimum courtesies.

Pleased, he enjoyed the rest of his ride and left the Professor in the care of Benson and Ape while he walked back into the house. The kitchen was a hive of activity, with several maids scurrying about under Cook's orders.

Upstairs, the entrance hall was bright and spotlessly clean, as was the staircase and the passage to his bedchamber. Bedchambers, plural, since without instruction, Mrs. Park had made up both the master chamber and the one opposite. He slept in the second room and dressed in the first. It worked for now.

In his new morning attire, he entered the breakfast parlour to delicious smells of bacon and sausage and freshly toasted bread, and a large pot of coffee. Newspapers, ironed and pristine, were laid on the table beside his place setting. He enjoyed a solitary if splendid breakfast, while he caught up with the news—more machine-breaking and other unrest in the north, while on the Peninsula, Badajoz was still under siege. Then he strolled out to keep his appointment in the library.

Ape was already there. Somewhat to Piers's surprise, Benson, a much older man, had come, too. Piers nodded to him in welcome and he gave a self-conscious grin.

"Never be a head groom if I can't read," Benson said.

"Sit," Piers invited. There were two tables in the room, and Piers quickly placed pencils and paper in front of each place at the larger. While he prepared, the door opened again and the younger footman called Francis came in, closely followed by the frightened scullery maid, whose name, he could just make out from her whisper, was Janey.

It was an interesting hour. He had never taught anyone such basics before and, apart from Ape, they were all clearly in awe of their master. But they were eager, and the first lesson passed very well, with everyone copying out their own names, and matching the letters with the sounds.

While he did so, he watched each of them, trying to find something about their appearance to latch onto for future recognition. Francis the footman wore livery and had small scar on his chin. Janey was small and skinny, with her apron wrapped almost completely around her. Benson was slightly grey and wearing outdoor clothes. Both he and Ape smelled of horse.

At ten, he praised them and sent them back to normal duties.

"I'll be wanting the curricle in half an hour," he told Benson.

"I'll bring it round."

"Can I come?" Ape demanded.

"Yes, I shall need you." He was aware of Ape's grin as he strode out. It seemed to contain something of relief, as though he had been afraid Piers might dismiss him now that he had a proper groom.

In fact, Ape was the knottiest of his problems and he had no real idea how to solve the issue.

Driving the greys, Piers's first stops were in Bond Street. At each, Ape leapt agilely down to hold the horses' heads, and even walk them up and down if Piers took too long.

As Piers called in at several tailors and bootmakers, a pattern quickly emerged. It seemed he owed a good deal of money for items he had never seen, bought, in fact, while he was still in Oxford. When he made it plain to the proprietors that they would be paid, but that from now on credit was limited to his person, they were all so relieved and apologetic that it was quite easy to inquire into the custom of one Mr. Henry Devon.

From there, he drove on to Piccadilly and St. James. Here, he was less sure of receiving answers. He was not a member of any of the gentlemen's clubs and neither the doormen nor any other staff were likely to give him the information he wanted.

He came to a halt outside White's, gazing thoughtfully at the front door.

"Here, mister?" Ape asked.

Was it worth it?

The front door opened, and a gentleman ran out, and down the steps, calling something humorous over his shoulder to the doorman. Piers frowned, because there was something familiar about this gentleman. Tall-ish, broad in the shoulder, black hair and dark, ugly-attractive features.

The man caught him gawping and halted abruptly. "Withy?" he said incredulously.

Abruptly, Piers jumped down from the curricle. "Haggs!" He flung out his hand to his old undergraduate friend, but the meeting seemed to be worth more than a mere handshake. With genuine pleasure, Piers absorbed the back and shoulder thumps, and got in a few of his own.

Fortunately, Ape was at the horses' heads, smiling approvingly as though his shy child had just made a suitable friend.

"What the devil are you doing in town?" Haggs demanded. "Never tell me you've escaped the alma mater?"

Piers grimaced. "Dragged out by the hair, kicking and screaming. I inherited my uncle's title."

Haggs blinked. "That must have been quite a run of bad luck. I'm sorry." Then he grinned. "Viscount, eh?"

"The very same. I have to say you look quite exceedingly the man about town."

"Oh, I am," Haggs said gravely, standing back to bow elaborately. "Sir Peter Haggard at your service. I inherited too."

This was not quite so unexpected since Haggs had been the previous baronet's eldest son.

"Sorry," Piers said sincerely. "Was it sudden?"

"Short illness. Two years ago. We should have kept in touch."

"We should. But I'm damned glad to run into you."

"Likewise," Haggs said. He nodded toward White's. "You going in for luncheon?"

"Not a member, sadly."

"I'll propose you if you like. Bound to get a second."

"Thanks. Yes, why not?" He hesitated, then said, "Actually, I'm looking into someone who's pursuing my cousin. I suspect he's a member here, but obviously I don't know the staff."

"I do," Haggs said. "Who's the bounder after your cousin? Fortune hunter?"

"I suspect so. Henry Devon?"

Haggs frowned. "Sindon's heir? Not a friend of his. But come on, we can ask Arthur."

Arthur was the doorman on duty, and under Haggs's beguiling questioning, he spilled a few salient facts, namely that Devon owed membership fees and a large bill.

"What you expected?" Haggs asked as they went back down the steps.

"Pretty much. Thanks, Haggs."

"Happy to help! Got an appointment now, but I'll meet up with you later, if you like."

"Come and dine," Piers said. "Got a wonderful new cook and it's a shame if she feeds only me."

"Happy to help again," Haggs assured him, and with a last wave, sauntered off.

Thoughtfully, Piers returned to the curricle, and gave Ape time to leap back onto his perch. He turned the horses for home.

"You're right," Ape said when they were away from the worst traffic noise. "That Devon's a bad 'un."

"How do you know?" Piers asked sceptically.

"Because when we met Miss Gussie in the park, she was frightened."

"Frightened?" Piers spared him a quick, frowning glance over his shoulder. He didn't ask the same question on the tip of his tongue again: *How do you know?* Because he was aware that Ape knew fear in most of its forms, something that made Piers's fingers tighten on the reins involuntary and caused the horses to toss their heads in annoyance. "In what way?" he asked at last.

He could almost see Ape shrugging. "Don't know. Maybe he's a bad driver. Or maybe he's all hands."

Or all threat of it.

"You should speak to her again," Ape said.

"I will."

That seemed to satisfy Ape, who lapsed back into silence. As though he trusted Piers to see to it. A couple of times, he turned quickly, as though to say something, and then apparently thought better of it, which bothered Piers. But one could not force trust.

During the afternoon, after another enlightening visit to Mr. Pepper the solicitor, Piers sustained a visit from Aunt Hortensia, with Gussie in tow.

"We are making calls and cannot stay," Hortensia said as he joined them in the drawing room. Hortensia was gazing around the room with some resentment, whether because it was no longer hers or because it was clean and well arranged by his new staff, he could not tell.

"Then I cannot interest you in tea?" Piers offered.

Aunt Hortensia shuddered. "Thank you, no. I have no idea what staff you have installed here, or what skills they have. Bertie says you have a street urchin as your groom!"

"Oh, the grooms don't make the tea," Piers said.

"You are being obtuse!"

"Not I, Aunt," he said delicately, and before she could do more than suspect the insult turned back on herself, he said, "Then how might I help you?"

"Don't be silly, Piers. We came to invite you to dine with us tonight."

"Thank you. I regret I am engaged this evening."

She stared at him in disbelief. "With what?"

"The entire opera company from Covent Garden, dropping over for a bacchanal."

Aunt Hortensia's face flushed unbecomingly. "Are you trying to be amusing, Piers?"

"No, I am trying to point out, in a light-hearted way, that it is absolutely none of your business."

Aunt Hortensia's mouth fell open. Beside her, even Gussie's laughing face had acquired a look of astonished unease. Hortensia tried to glare him down, but he held her gaze, faintly smiling, until Gussie rushed into speech.

"Actually, he is right, Mama. What about tomorrow evening, Cousin? Or are you promised to the Haymarket Theatre company?"

"Tomorrow, I shall be delighted to dine."

Aunt Hortensia nodded curtly and sailed out of the room. Piers chose to walk downstairs with them, so that as Gussie walked blithely out and over to the waiting carriage, he could detain her mother in private.

"A moment, aunt," he said on the step. "How serious are you about encouraging Henry Devon to offer for Gussie?"

"That," she snapped, "is absolutely none of *your* business."

"Actually, it is. I am her guardian, and the question stands."

"Oh, for goodness sake, Piers, what do you know of the world? It would be a fine feather in Augusta's cap, securing such a fine match in her first season and you would be unkind to deny her it just to be perverse!"

"Do you know anything about his circumstances? His family?"

"I know both intimately," she said grandly. "His mother is my closest friend."

"I see," Piers said. There was no point in suggesting she chaperone Gussie more closely or send a maid or footman with her when she went out with Devon. As a matter of course, she discounted everything he said.

He watched them go, then asked the footman for his hat and walked round to the Gadsby house in Mount Street.

Maria was at home, but entertaining morning callers. Fortunately, for purposes of quick recognition, she rose to welcome him, looking somewhat flummoxed to see him, but welcoming enough. She presented several people he knew he would never remember again and introduced him with perfect propriety as "my cousin, Lord Petteril."

"Ah, you are newly arrived in London, I hear," one lady said. "Being such a friend of your family, I took the liberty of sending you a card for my ball next week. I hope you will come."

Ah, so this was Lady Amberly. He had indeed received a card, though he hadn't got as far as formally declining.

"Thank you for that kindness. I am trying to work out whether or not it would be kindness on my part to accept."

"Why would it not be?" asked the young lady beside Lady Amberly. Miss Amberly presumably.

"I don't dance," Piers said apologetically. "What use at a ball is a guest who does not dance?"

Several people were gazing at him in astonishment.

"You don't dance?" Miss Amberly repeated. "Whyever not?"

Because he had very little chance of recognizing those he had invited to do so. "It is an affliction," he said sadly.

One of the gentlemen laughed. "You are a card, my lord!"

In fact, apart from the Amberlys, most of Maria's callers were gentlemen, who seemed to be vying for her attention while, of course, never neglecting the Amberlys. Everyone left in ones or twos shortly after Piers's arrival, finally leaving him alone with his cousin.

"Did you want to see Jeremy?" she asked, apparently at a loss as to why he was still here. "I believe he is at his club."

"I'd like to talk to him at some point, but actually it is you I came to speak to this afternoon."

"Oh? What about?"

"Gussie. Or more precisely, Henry Devon."

"She does seem very taken with him, as we said before. And he is quite a catch, you know."

"In personal terms? Or material ones?"

Maria laughed. "Both, silly. I told you, he is Lord Sindon's heir. Sindon is very wealthy. His land is in the north, but he has other interests all over the country—mills and shipping and such—which is no doubt where the real money comes from, though of course no one will admit it. Mama has known them forever. She and Lady Sindon are forever corresponding."

"Then Lord and Lady Sindon are not in town?"

"Oh, no. They have never been that I can recall. In fact, I have never met them."

"I suppose that explains why Sindon keeps his heir so short."

"Short?" Maria asked, bewildered.

"Of funds. Devon owes money all over town."

She waved that aside with no interest. "Oh, well, you know what young men are."

"I know what *some* men are, of whatever age. Gadsby isn't in trouble, is he?"

"Jeremy?" She looked startled, then defensive. "Of course not. What sort of trouble could he possibly be in?"

"Oh, financial, debts, that kind of thing."

She laughed so insincerely that he knew not to expect the truth. "Of course not! Piers, you don't have to worry about us all. And Mama knows what she is doing with Devon."

"Does she? Do *you* like him?"

"He would not do for me, but he is fun, like Gussie. They get up to mischief together."

"Such as?"

"Oh, childish things, like telling Mama they are going driving in the park and going somewhere else entirely."

He gazed at her. "And that does not trouble you?"

A hint of colour seeped into her pale, perfect skin. "No. It might, were it anyone not known to us. But the Sindons are my parents' closest friends and Henry is their son."

"The Sindons, whom no one has seen in the—what? —five-and-twenty years of your life?"

"What are you implying, Piers?" she asked with a first note of alarm.

"That Gussie is seventeen years old and mischievous by nature. That she finds Devon exciting but doesn't really know how to deal with him. That at some point he has frightened her, and she doesn't know whether that is silly or not."

Maria's mouth fell open.

"You don't need to believe me," Piers said. "Your mother certainly would not. So, I ask you only to keep a closer eye on her. Go with her to the park. Encourage her to take her maid. Be sure she is *actually* chaperoned at parties."

Maria opened her mouth, no doubt to defend her mother and her sister, then closed it again, perhaps remembering incidents of laxness or complacency.

"Tell me something else," Piers said, "Did you ever have spare keys to Petteril House?"

She blinked but answered readily enough. "We did for a while. Mama left them, though she took them back again before you came to London. You didn't need to change the locks, you know."

"I rather think I did. The necklace vanished and there appear to be keys all over the city."

She lifted her chin. "Bertie said you were burgled."

"Not with keys, though, and the necklace had already gone."

"How do you *know* your burglars didn't take it?" she challenged.

He rose and smiled. "Because I looked through the loot. Thanks for the tea, coz. Goodbye."

Chapter Nine

Miss Augusta Withan was enjoying her first Season so much that she rarely remembered her odd moments of confusion. However, at Mrs. Harcourt's musical soiree that evening, one such moment hit her with unexpected and not quite pleasant force.

She had not expected to see Henry there—he didn't really care for music—so the sight of him sauntering in late and greeting his hostess with his usual charm should have made her giddy with happiness. Instead, she felt a cold twinge in her belly, a consciousness that she had not really wanted to see him.

Which was silly. She was in love with him, was she not?

Well, even married people did not want to spend *every* moment together. Look at Maria and Jeremy. But Gussie was not quite ready to look forward to her beloved's absence. She wanted her heart to sing as it had used to, and she wasn't quite sure why it did not.

She decided to stick uncharacteristically close to her mother, which was fine while the violinist played his exquisite piece, but recoiled on her immediately afterward when her mother led her straight to Henry's side without giving her a chance to flit off to her own friends.

"Lady Petteril," he greeted her mother with a bow, and a special smile for Gussie. "Miss Withan."

"We thought you were not coming," Hortensia said archly.

"Oh, I didn't mean to." His eyes gleamed at Gussie. "But I could not resist. Might I fetch you some refreshment, ladies? Wine or lemonade?"

"Oh, nothing for me, thank you. I must just congratulate Mrs. Harcourt on her superb violinist..."

"Well, did *you* find him superb?" Gussie asked Henry as her mother abandoned her.

"Frankly, it hurt my ears," Henry replied with a boyish grin. "But I braved it for you."

"I'm flattered."

"You know I adore you. And yet you were so cold to me yesterday."

"Because I chose to go in my cousin's curricle for ten minutes?" she scoffed. "You would have delighted in such horses. Why shouldn't I, since I had the chance?"

"Because you chose him over my adventure."

"Where's the adventure in galloping about the streets?"

He leaned closer, his breath stirring her hair for an instant, causing an echo of that thrill she had first felt with him. "Because we could have stopped somewhere quiet, and I could have kissed you."

She flushed, but he had already moved decorously back, offering her his arm. She took it but decided to retrieve control of the entire situation. "I don't mind the kisses," she said, outrageously brazen. "It's the pawing I object to."

At the word pawing, a spurt of anger flashed in his eyes and vanished into a more indulgent mockery. "My little innocent. You are thinking of Petteril House. A more sophisticated lady would have rejoiced in my caresses."

Gussie suspected that a more sophisticated lady would have known not to enter an empty house with him whatever the dare. "It was foolish. My cousin arrived only hours afterward."

"Don't fret. I'll charm your cousin, too."

She looked at him with distaste. "With what purpose? You imagine he will lend you his house to ravish his cousin?"

This time she had the satisfaction of having appalled him. "Keep your voice down," he said nervously.

She laughed. "Oh, Henry, who is unsophisticated now?" She helped herself to lemonade from the table and, dropping his arm, flitted off to join her particular friends.

Ape came home quite late again after another quite interesting but less dangerous evening. Mr. Park was just about to lock the back door when Ape slipped inside.

"You should be in bed, my lad," Mr. Park said severely. "This is getting to be a habit, and one neither Benson nor I will put up with. You can't just wander off when you like."

"I know, but I need to tell himself something. Is he still up?"

Park sighed. "He's with a guest in the dining room."

"Still?" Ape said disapprovingly. "Are they bosky?"

Mr. Park looked down his nose, but Ape wasn't fooled. The butler's eyes were trying very hard not to laugh.

Ape grinned openly. "I'll nip up and see for myself."

"Grooms don't go into the house unless summoned," Mr. Park pointed out. At the same time, he made no effort to stop Ape sliding toward the stairs. Which was interesting. Maybe he was looking for an excuse to dismiss Ape. Maybe his lordship was.

It made his stomach twinge, but it didn't stop him. After all, giving his lordship information might sweeten him up.

The dining room smelled of wine, but not thickly like the stale stink of old ale and gin. Not like the Silver Jug, or the Queen's Head. The remains of their meal had been cleared away. Only glasses and two decanters remained. Lord Petteril had slouched right back in his chair, his feet resting on the table. Ape had never seen him so relaxed, or, with laughter playing around his eyes and mouth, so...handsome. Which caused Ape's stomach another twinge, although this one was not unpleasant.

His guest, Haggs—Sir Peter Haggard—was not handsome, but there was something attractive about his harsh, big-boned face and the casual way he lounged two places away from his lordship, with one foot up on the chair between.

Lord Petteril's fingers—long and fine and smooth, a gentleman's hands, used to books and writing and decent gloves to keep out the cold—curled around the stem of his elegant glass. He began to raise it to his lips, then blinked as he spotted Ape in the doorway.

Abruptly, his feet slipped off the table and he sat up, like a naughty child caught by his mother. "Ape?"

He didn't sound like anyone's mother. Haggs turned his head in surprise. "Tyger, tyger, burning bright," he drawled, incomprehensibly.

Ape ignored him. "Are you bosky, mister, I mean my lord? Or can I have a word?"

Lord Petteril waved him to the chair on his other side, opposite Haggs. "Word away."

Ape didn't move. "It's private. About that cove we don't like. From the park."

"Ah, that cove. In that case, definitely sit down. Sir Peter is in my confidence. Haggs, this is Ape, tiger and groom in training."

Reluctantly, Ape walked in. He had experience of men in their cups, and they were bloody unpredictable. Still, he'd trusted his lordship this far.

Ape sat. "I went to a tavern this evening."

Lord Petteril scowled. "Did you go back to St. Giles?"

"Don't be daft. No point, is there? I followed Devon's servant to his favoured alehouse near where we met *him*." He jerked his head at Sir Peter Haggard. "And I listened."

Lord Petteril's eyes, a little softened by wine and the good humour of friendship, were nevertheless alarmingly alert. "Did you, by God? What did you hear?"

"That the Devons ain't rich at all. Land's failing and Lord Sindon is all to pieces. Rumour of all the Sindon wealth comes from our man's mam, Lady Sindon, who pretends to all her friends in letters 'cause she never comes to London, *and* from Henry Devon's servant who strung a few more lies to other servants when they first came to town. On his master's bidding."

"Could be done," Haggard allowed.

"And the servant just blabbed to all his friends about this in the tavern?" Lord Petteril said with more scepticism.

"No. He was drunk as a wheelbarrow and confided to one cove, only his voice was too loud, and my ears is sharp."

"They are," Lord Petteril allowed. "So is your brain. Well done."

"Also," Ape went on, refraining from preening with a small amount of effort. "This Devon is after a particular heiress to solve his problems, who I think must be your cousin."

"She's got some decent settlements on her marriage," Petteril said.

Ape had no idea what that meant but he took it as agreement. "The servant was sneering because Devon had thought he could charm the girl into marriage and now might have to abduct her, and I don't think you should let him."

Haggard sat up.

"No," Lord Petteril said slowly. "No, I don't think I should either. My thanks, Ape. I doubt you should have been there, but I'm rather glad you were."

Ape felt his cheeks burn with pleasure. Fortunately, Lord Petteril's mind was still on the problem of his cousin.

"There must be richer girls in town," he mused, "but I suppose speed is of the essence to Devon before anyone finds out he's pockets to let. And misrepresenting himself to boot."

Haggard was gazing at him with amusement. "When did *you* become so worldly wise?"

"Oh, I'm not, just paying attention," his lordship said vaguely.

Ape jerked his head toward Haggard. "Does *he* know about the missing article?"

"I mentioned it in passing."

Ape wasn't sure how he felt about that. His instinct was to approve of Sir Peter Haggard, and he was glad that his lordship had what appeared to be a good friend he could rely on. On the other hand, he couldn't quite help the twist of resentment that he was not Petteril's only ally anymore. Which was just plain daft because lords didn't regard scum like Ape as friends. Ever. He should remember that.

Forcing his mind back to the matter in hand, Ape said, "Do you think Devon managed to steal the necklace? Or got Miss Gussie to do it for him?"

"It crossed my mind," Lord Petteril said slowly. "I'm trying to dismiss it because I like Gussie, but I have to consider it. There were several sets of keys to this place taken to Half Moon Street, and certainly for a time there was one set in the Gadsbys' house, too. Gussie, or even Devon—depending on where the keys actually were—could have borrowed them and put them back later when the deed was done."

"My money's on Devon," Haggard said. "On the grounds that I don't like him."

"I don't like any of 'em," Ape said. "Not the bosky bloke from Tatt's who's married to your other cousin, and not that smarmy officer who swaggers about like he's Lord Wellington or the Prince Regent."

"Gadsby and Bertie?" Haggard guessed, glancing from Ape to Lord Petteril. "Does he get to speak of his betters like that?"

"Can't stop him," Lord Petteril said, his mind clearly on something more important. Ape felt his face flush, part shame for showing Petteril up, and part anger with Haggard for pointing it out. "Besides, who says they are?"

"Are what?" Haggard asked in brief confusion, setting down his glass.

"Better," said Petteril. "We know the old butler, Herries, gave his set of keys to Bertie. Hortensia, my aunt, must have the housekeeper's. Hortensia could have used them herself. In fact, she did, the day after I arrived in London. And Gussie, Maria, Gadsby, and Devon, could all have borrowed them."

Haggard's eyebrows flew up. "You suspect *Lady Petteril?*"

"She's a ruthless old besom," Petteril said frankly. "Though she is devoted to the family's good name, so I can't understand why she would dispose of an heirloom like the necklace."

"To stop you having it," Ape suggested.

"Possible. Or to help one of the others."

"What motive would the others have?" Haggard asked. "Pockets to let like Devon?"

"Pretty much, though Maria denied it. She might not know. And Bertie will want promotion which he probably can't afford."

Ape scowled. "We need to find the necklace. You got to let me go back to the Silver Jug. Just for an hour. I can look after myself. Always have."

"I know," Petteril said, focusing on him. "And you saved my bacon in St. Giles too. Thing is, the necklace isn't there. Never was."

Ape's jaw dropped. "You went there without me!"

"I did, and I was very glad to get out again. Who's your money on, Ape?"

"As the thief?" Ape said, reluctantly distracted from alarm and indignation. "The captain. On the grounds," he added, with a quick, cheeky grin at Haggard, "that I don't like him. But what we need to do, if the necklace ain't sold it, is search their stuff and find it."

Lord Petteril sighed. "Tempting as it is, not sure my authority as head of the family will stretch that far."

"I could crack their kens," Ape offered, though he wasn't surprised when his lordship scowled him down. He drew in his breath and blurted, "I already looked in Captain Withan's rooms and he ain't got it there."

The scowl grew fixed though Petteril seemed to be speechless. "Don't," he uttered at last.

"If you go to confront them, I'd come with you and guard your back," Haggard said to Petteril. "Thing is, you'd be burning your bridges."

"What bridges?" Ape asked, confused.

"He means any chance of friendship with my family," Lord Petteril said.

Ape didn't ask him if he cared. He knew he didn't want to think about it, and Ape could understand that too.

Petteril picked up his glass and took a mouthful before turning his thoughtful gaze on Ape. "Away to bed, lad. You've been of great help this evening, but you have an early start in the morning. Don't wake Benson up and don't forget to bolt the stable door."

Ape bounced up. At the door, he remembered to bow, though he hadn't quite wiped the smile off his face.

Haggard said thoughtfully, "*Did he smile his work to see? Did he who made the Lamb make thee?*"

"I find Blake impenetrable enough when I'm sober," Piers said. "In the words of my tiger, button it."

"Your tiger is my inspiration, Withy." Haggs fixed him with a stare, his expression veiled. "You do realize he's a girl?"

Petteril sighed. It was a relief in a way. "Yes, and I don't know what to do about it. I can't have him sleeping with the grooms. Or the maids. He'd make a terrible maid. And in any case, he's more comfortable as a boy."

"Why?"

"I expect it's safer in St. Giles." He thought about it, remembering the man who'd grabbed Ape in the Silver Jug. "Marginally. He grew up with no one to look after him except prostitutes and thieves. I don't know how or where he learned his honour, but he has it." His lips quirked. "*She* has it."

"How old is she?"

"I have no idea. Older than the ten I took him for when I thought he was a boy. He wears that baggy jacket to cover his shape, even though he's got a better one. My guess is somewhere between fourteen and eighteen."

"Do you mean to keep her in your household?"

"Or safe in someone else's. But she has a lot of learning to do to become a girl again. If she even wants to."

Haggs scratched his head. "Not sure there's an option. Servants live on top of each other, without much in the way of privacy. Sooner or later, the secret will come out. And just imagine the scandal that will be made of it. *Lord Petteril disguised his tiger as a boy so he could take her everywhere he—*"

"Stop it," Petteril said angrily. "I know what they'll say, and I don't want that for him. Her. She's suffered enough. I just don't know how to fix it. Yet."

Haggs reached over and poured some more brandy into his own glass, and then into Piers's. "You will do, my friend. You will do. In the meantime, one more brandy for the road, and then I must go."

Chapter Ten

Piers's reunion with Haggs left him with a slightly thick head the following morning. However, several cups of coffee, a quick, solitary gallop in the park with the Professor, followed by a decent breakfast, and he felt much more human. By nine, he was ready to continue his reading lessons, and glad to see all his pupils return.

He had no idea how the lessons were regarded by the rest of the household, though he was given one clue when a knock on the door heralded the arrival of Joshua, the first footman with a silver tray on which lay several letters and a small packet.

Curiosity, Piers thought with a hint of amusement, for the post was normally left on a table in the front hall for him to see whenever he passed.

Piers, who had been helping Janey the scullery maid at that moment, straightened, and stepped back as Joshua approached.

"Thank you," Piers said, lifting the handful from the tray, and noting that all work had stopped. Francis the footman wriggled uncomfortably in his seat. Janey dropped her pencil. Only Ape paid no attention, his—her—lips moving silently as she pronounced the letters in her head. Piers held Joshua's gaze. "In future, you may leave the post in the hall as I requested."

Joshua at least had the grace to flush. He bowed and walked quickly away, remembering to close the door behind him.

"Write your names again as neatly as you can, and show me before you go," Piers said.

While they obeyed, he flicked through the post, which was largely cards of invitation. The packet intrigued him, so using the paper knife from the other desk, he cut into it and emptied out a glittering pile of gold and red.

Slowly he lifted it. A necklace made up of gold chains and two strands of elegant little rubies.

Dropping the necklace into his palm, he closed his fingers around it and looked up to find Ape staring at him, mouth agape.

"Cor," she said.

Cor indeed.

There was no note in the packet to say where or who it had come from, so it was not that someone had sent the necklace to be cleaned and forgotten about it. The direction on the wrapping was in plain, large letters, probably to disguise the hand of the writer.

Piers pocketed both necklace and wrapping, and forced himself to concentrate on his students, who had all remembered the letters of their names and written them with varying degrees of legibility.

"Well done," he said cheerfully. "More tomorrow."

Inevitably, Ape lingered, pretending to finish up while the others left the room. "Is that what I think it is?"

"A very good question," Piers said, extracting the necklace from his pocket and holding it up to the light. "It would certainly appear to be. Tell Benson I want the curricle. And yourself, of course."

"Where we going?" Ape asked eagerly.

"Ludgate Hill," Piers replied. Where could be found the largest concentration of reputable—and discreet—goldsmiths and jewellers in London.

A swift rummage through the vast collection of old invoices in the ground floor office provided Piers with the name of the jeweller most favoured by his uncle, appropriately named Golding and Son. So, it was there he made his first stop, leaving Ape in charge of the horses.

Since he was "in twig" as the viscount, the assistant promptly deserted his current, more ordinary customer and approached Piers, all but rubbing his hands together with glee.

"Good morning, sir. What might we help you with today?" He was a smartly dressed young man with oiled hair.

"Please, serve your other customer first. I expect to take up quite a bit of your time."

The assistant clearly would have preferred to dismiss the other customer, but a quick glance at the older, scowling man in the workshop behind, had him scurrying back to his duty.

The older man emerged from the back of the shop, limping. "Perhaps I can help you, sir?"

"I hope so. My name is..." From habit, he almost said Withan. He smiled faintly and reached for the new cards he had had printed for him. "Petteril."

The man barely glanced at the card, but his eyes widened considerably. "My lord! I'm Golding. I had the honour to serve your...uncle, I think? The previous viscount?"

"Indeed. It is on account of his patronage that I have come first to you with my inquiry."

"A discreet inquiry, my lord? Perhaps you would step into the back room?"

Part workshop, part office with a comfortable chair for favoured visitors, the room was bright with sunlight from two windows. Piers took the comfortable chair with thanks, and as Mr. Golding sat down opposite, he drew the necklace from his pocket and passed it across the table between them.

"What would be your assessment of its worth, Mr. Golding?"

Golding clamped an eyepiece into his eye and examined the jewels minutely. Then he picked up a magnifying glass, a bigger version of the quizzing glasses dangling from Piers's neck.

Golding laid down the glass, let the eyepiece fall, and sat back in his chair. "The gold is worth something, but the rubies are paste."

Piers sighed. "I thought so. I don't suppose you were commissioned to make this?"

"No, nor sell the originals. I take it this *should* be the Petteril necklace?"

"Indeed. Is the gold the original?"

"It looks to be. It's old and finely wrought. The paste rubies are pretty well made, too. And with the charm of the old gold, most people would never suspect the rubies were not real. It is nicely done. But not by me."

"Is it too much to hope you recognize the work?" Piers asked.

Golding examined the stones again. "Yes," he said apologetically. "But perhaps I could narrow it down for you a little." Seizing a piece of paper, he scribbled down several names, and handed the paper to Piers. "And if you manage to locate the actual rubies, I shall be happy to replace them for you. It is an exquisite piece."

"It was," Piers said wryly. "And hopefully will be again. Thank you, Mr. Golding. You have been most helpful, and I shall remember it."

The rest of the morning was spent ambling up and down the hill in search of Golding's names and making enquiries in each shop. On these enquiries, Piers did not offer his name or his card, merely mentioned that he was looking to have some jewels made for a very special lady. Here, he either looked coy or winked, depending on his perception of the jeweller he spoke to. He said the lady loved rubies and he was looking for a particular shape and gradation of sizes in the stones. He was shown several, none of which he found satisfactory.

On the fourth visit, he detected a gleam in the jeweller's eye that made his heartbeat faster. He was again invited into the back room and a perfect array of rubies was set out before him.

"I have just recently acquired them, sir," Mr. Ellis said reverently. "I've been waiting for that special customer who would appreciate such ageless beauty, such exquisite cutting."

"You did not cut them yourself, Mr. Ellis?" Piers raised his quizzing glass and examined one of the stones, then another.

"No, sir, but they are clearly the work of a master. Exquisite. Unique."

"Indeed?" Piers let his quizzing glass fall and reached into his pocket. He spread the necklace among his fingers, revealing the paste rubies of identical cut.

Ellis paled, his mouth dropping open, his eyes lifting slowly from the necklace to Piers's face. "Where did you get that, sir?" he asked hoarsely.

"From you, I imagine. Indirectly. I'm Petteril."

"Aren't you happy with the work, sir? I mean, my lord?" Ellis said anxiously. "Her ladyship seemed very pleased indeed."

"Her ladyship," Piers repeated with a sigh. "Lady Petteril."

"Indeed, sir. Lovely lady of impeccable taste."

"Oh undoubtedly. Of doubtful sense, however. How much did you give her for the rubies?"

Five minutes later, he emerged from Ellis's shop. Passing Ape, he opened his pocket to allow a swift glimpse. Ape looked up, clear blue eyes gleaming with admiration.

"Cor," Piers said and strode past the horses to jump up on the curricle.

"So, it was old Lady Petteril all along," Ape said in tones of awe. Still on his perch, he had twisted round to talk to Piers once they had left the busiest streets for the quieter, residential squares of Mayfair.

"Perhaps," Piers said doubtfully. "Admittedly, I am somewhat blind to faces, but would you, Ape, describe her ladyship as *a lovely lady*?"

"Gawd, no," Ape said fervently.

Piers, glancing over his shoulder, saw Ape watching him from under drooping eyelids, as though wondering whether or not to apologize for his disparaging if sincere comment.

Piers faced the way his horses were going. "I think all we can say is that it was someone calling herself Lady Petteril who sold the rubies to Ellis and got him to make paste replacements for the necklace."

"One of your cousins?" Ape sounded as disappointed as Piers felt. "If it was Miss Gussie, I bet she did it for Devon."

Which would certainly explain her odd mix of flirtation and discomfort around her suitor. And either of them could have taken the keys to steal the necklace. Or they could have done it together.

"If she did, I expect that would be true. But it doesn't need to have been either Maria or Gussie. I'm sure Bertie and Gadsby—and Devon, come to that—are well acquainted with women who are quite capable of playing the part of a Lady Petteril for half an hour's negotiation."

Ape swore. "Then we're no further forward!"

"You'd better not say those words in front of Mrs. Park. In fact, don't say them at all. As for being further forward, we have the rubies back, and Mr. Golding will return them to the necklace."

"And how're you going to get your money back?" Ape demanded.

"I'm probably not," Piers admitted. "Or at least not directly."

"And you still don't know who not to trust!"

Piers lips twisted. "Oh, I don't trust any of them."

Over a light luncheon, Piers forced himself to examine the estate books and correspondence, since these would be his next matter of business. While he was so occupied, Joshua entered and presented him with a note.

"Hand delivered, my lord."

"Are they waiting for an answer?" Piers asked unfolding the unsealed, undirected missive.

"No, my lord." Joshua bowed and departed, and Piers read the short, impersonal missive from Hortensia, who addressed him merely as nephew and signed herself Hortensia Petteril. The jist of it was that she was postponing his dinner invitation, on the grounds of a sudden sick headache.

Piers wondered if her headache had anything to do with a word from Mr. Ellis, either to her or anyone she was in league with. On the other hand, he could have sworn her surprise at not finding the necklace that first morning was genuine, although admittedly he had not been at his best to observe. Perhaps someone had confessed to her.

If so, things were coming to a head.

After staring blindly out of the window for some time, he sent for Ape.

"You know Devon's residence, I believe."

"He's got lodgings off Piccadilly."

"Can you watch him discreetly? Follow him and tell me if he goes anywhere he's likely to meet my cousin?"

"Sure," Ape said at once.

"My aunt is indisposed, or claiming to be, so she won't be chaperoning Gussie, and knowing that little minx, she'll use the opportunity to get up to mischief. I'll be here until six, then I'm going to White's to dine. Whether or not anything happens, I want you back here before ten. Understood?"

"I ain't stupid."

"I'll take that as obedience. Shab off."

Ape grinned and bounced out, so glad to be useful that Piers couldn't help smiling, even though it ended as something rather more like a grimace.

Piers entered White's as Haggard's guest. Haggs had already put his name forward and it had been seconded by a friend of Piers's late brother Ivor. His admission to the club was really no more than a formality, everyone assured him as they came up to greet him and exchange a few words. The older men respected his name and title and were happy to recall his father and uncle. The younger seemed to regard him as a likeable curiosity.

He tried his best to find some means of matching men to names—a small scar, extremely pale eyes, carroty-red hair—but even so, he knew he would meet most of them as a stranger the next time too. So, he made a point of saying, as he had done so often at Oxford, that he had a shockingly bad memory, and maintaining a certain aloofness so that when they did meet again, it would not be quite so obvious exactly how shocking his memory was.

Only while dining with Haggs under the vaulted ceiling of White's hallowed dining room, did he wonder why he bothered even to try and hide the affliction. A personal tendency toward civility, perhaps. Combined with the odd contemptuous backhander from his father and the ridicule of his brother and cousins. The funny thing was, his family seemed to have forgotten those incidents. Only Piers remembered.

"What about the unspeakable Devon?" Haggs asked quietly. "How do you plan to spike his guns?"

"I'm rather hoping to have him arrested for stealing the necklace. But I suppose that would be too good to be true. In the meantime, I have Ape watching him. Tomorrow night is the Amberley ball, is it not? I'd appreciate what help you can give me keeping an eye on him there. I've asked my cousin Maria to keep a closer watch on her sister, because my aunt seems so determined on the match that she almost pushes Gussie into Devon's arms."

Haggs nodded, but as he swallowed the last of his beef and laid down his knife and fork, a gleam of amusement shone in his eyes. "Who'd have thought it? Piers Withan playing propriety."

"I am a very proper person. In the proper places."

Haggs made a derisive noise. "Brandy? Port?"

"Why don't we take a brandy and stroll around the card rooms?"

"Why don't we indeed."

Piers did not play but had some hopes of observing Bertie or Gadsby or even Devon at the tables. However, none of them appeared to be present at the club that evening, and there was no gossip either. He did mention a couple of times that he believed his cousins were members here, but neither direct conversation nor shameless eavesdropping elicited any useful information.

Of course, they would be members of other clubs, too, some of them on the much less respectable side. Piers, who found cards and dice pretty dull, felt his heart sink at the prospect of hanging around in gaming hells. Maybe he should simply *talk* to them.

There was the seed of an idea there...

Haggs nudged him and he hastily followed his friend's gaze toward two men who had just entered the room and were walking between the tables. One of them was Maria's husband, Sir Jeremy Gadsby—Piers was familiar enough with him now to pick him out. He and his companion were conversing together, and yet their very posture told Piers there was no love lost between them. He read stiffness, dislike, and, as he strolled nearer, even anger.

Neither of them noticed Piers. The stranger's low, intense words were almost inaudible, but passing by, Piers caught something that sounded like, "...of honour—"

And then Gadsby cut him off, so furiously that his voice rose. "I'm aware! You needn't dun me like a damned tradesman." And strode away, throwing himself down at the nearest table.

His companion, tight-lipped, walked in the opposite direction.

So Gadsby owed at least one debt of honour. Though why gambling debts to already rich men should be regarded as more honourable to pay than debts to a struggling tradesman had always puzzled Piers.

But if Gadsby was the one who had sold the rubies, exchanging them for the fake stones in the necklace, would he not already have *paid* his debt of honour? Such talk as Piers had overheard could ruin a gentleman. It seemed, at last, that he could rule out one of his suspects.

In Covent Garden, Bertie Withan, in amorous pursuit of a generous widow, was annoyed to see his cousins Maria and Gussie arrive in the box almost directly opposite. One could not be too obviously outrageous under the observing eyes of one's female relatives. Were they not supposed to be dining with the unspeakable Piers tonight?

The ladies were escorted by Delby, one of Maria's devoted court of admirers, but if Piers was with them, too, he was hiding. But then, neither was there any sign of Aunt Hortensia. Grinning to himself, Bertie wished Piers and Hortensia joy of each other. But at the first interval, despite the risks of abandoning his widow to the blandishments of other men, curiosity drove him along the passage to his cousins' box.

"Good evening, cousins!" he greeted them cheerfully, nodding to Delby. "Where's the other one? The glorious head of our illustrious house?"

"If you mean Petteril, I have no idea," Maria said irritably. "Mama was forced to cancel dinner, so Augusta came out with me instead."

"What happened to my aunt?" he asked in surprise.

"Just a headache, but she cannot abide company in such a state."

"I don't blame her. I'd have had a headache, too."

Maria regarded him, frowning, "Why don't you like Piers? He's perfectly amiable."

"He may be the best of good fellows for all I care. He's in my way."

"That's not really his fault anymore that it is yours," Maria said thoughtfully. "He certainly doesn't want the honour. On the other hand, he seems to be dealing with the disappointment rather better."

Bertie, to his annoyance felt a flush rise into his face. "I imagine it's easier to deal with disappointment when one has land and wealth."

"I think you'd deal with it better if you weren't so pointlessly jealous," Gussie observed, adding before he could verbally annihilate her, "Who is the lady in your box?"

Bertie laughed.

Maria said hastily, "No one you will ever meet or mention."

"A lady who has done me a considerable favour," Bertie said mockingly. "I hope to return it one day. I don't see Devon here tonight."

It was meant to be a swipe at Gussie whose tongue was growing somewhat too impudent, but if she felt the barb, she gave no sign of it.

"Dining with friends, I think. Why, did you want him?"

"Do you expect me to bring him up to scratch?"

"Don't be vulgar, Bertie," Maria drawled. "Mr. Delby, do you go to the Amberlys' ball tomorrow evening?"

Bertie, feeling vaguely dissatisfied with himself and his cousins, took himself back to his widow who, in the end, proved to be very generous indeed. Again.

Chapter Eleven

"He didn't go out in the afternoon," Ape reported to Lord Petteril in the library that evening. "The valet did, for about an hour, but I thought I should stick with Devon."

"Quite right," Petteril approved.

"His nibs went out early in the evening, and I followed him to another of those gentlemen's clubs. Brooks? Hung around there for a couple of hours, waiting. He ain't a member, he was just the guest of some other nob, I learned that much. Then he went home again. If you ask me, he was scrounging his dinner."

"Sounds like it," Petteril agreed. "Did he go out again?"

"Not while I was there, and I was home by ten," Ape said virtuously.

Ape liked the way his lordship's lips twitched when he didn't want to laugh. Sometimes, you could encourage him with a grin, or even the twinkle of an eye. It was good to see him smile, warmed Ape's heart. He didn't smile now, though he didn't seem to be unhappy either. Instead, his eyes were uncomfortably penetrating, which gave Ape a bad moment.

"You must be cold," Lord Petteril said abruptly.

"Lot of standing around in the dark," Ape replied, by way of agreement. Just for a moment, he thought his lordship was going to tell him to sit by the fire, and his heart constricted with the anticipation of spending just a few more minutes with him in cosy companionship.

"Go down to the kitchen and get warm," Petteril ordered. "Have a hot drink before bed."

It was too obvious even to be disappointed. Lords didn't hob-nob of an evening with their servants. Ape laughed at himself, even as he summoned a grin for his employer. "Sure. Will you want me to watch Devon again tomorrow?"

"I'll let you know," Lord Petteril said so distantly that Ape's heart shrank with a thousand different fears and confused emotions, all of which were miserable and concerned being sent away.

By the time he had dressed for the Amberly ball, Henry Devon's plans were well laid. He'd had to send his man, Larson, out yesterday to arrange the post-chaise, which had given him no time to refill his sadly empty coffers. No matter. He had travelled on tick before, even without the heiress in tow.

And he could not risk waiting longer. Lord Petteril, Augusta's cousin and guardian, was poking into his affairs—which was more than her mother or brother-in-law had done—and sooner or later his lordship was liable to find out the truth not just about him but about the Sindon estate in general. Why the rest of the Withans regarded Petteril as dim and unworldly was beyond Devon. It was more vital than ever that any rumour be silenced, and once little Gussie was Devon's wife, none of her family, even the viscount, would dare reveal the truth.

Annoyingly, Gussie herself had not proved the soft touch he had hoped for either— neither quite enthralled enough nor willing enough to be compromised so that he might have had some hold over her family. There was only one solution left, and she would come round to it quickly enough. All women did.

Devon regarded himself in the glass from the top of his head—hair fashionably cut and arranged in the Brutus style—over his high, starched shirt points, perfectly folded cravat with its single diamond pin—all he had left of value—and his immaculate black evening coat and satin knee breeches. He nodded with self-satisfaction.

"Perfect, sir," Larson said, "if I may say so."

"You may," Devon said amiably. "So long as you make sure to get all our things out of here this evening, without being seen. And you must be with the chaise by midnight. If my bride proves shy, I may need help to keep her quiet just at first. Though let us pray not."

"Indeed, sir," Larson said piously.

Piers spent most of the day doing what he did best: thinking. About the necklace, his family, Ape, and what kind of a man he wanted to be.

By the time he dined in solitary informality, and went to change into his new evening clothes, he had more or less decided on a plan of action. It was not fixed, of course, or universally pleasing to him, and he still brooded upon it.

"My lord?" his valet said anxiously.

He blinked, having almost forgotten he had a valet now. Stewart was Scottish, young—not yet thirty—and so silent that Piers tended to forget he was there, discovering only later that his sleeve buttons were fastened and his coat being held for him. "Yes?"

"Is the pin satisfactory?"

Piers regarded the plain gold pin in the elegant, snowy folds of his cravat. "I suppose you think I should have more than one?"

"You might get bored, my lord."

Piers's eyes focused on his valet's bland face in the glass. Was that humour or sly insolence? "Heaven forfend. If it bores me, I'll have you pin a rose or a bunch of violets over the top. My coat, if you please."

It was definitely humour. He glimpsed it in the man's eyes before he lowered them and whisked away to fetch the coat. Perhaps he would do after all.

"You needn't wait up," Piers said, by way of reward. "I can undress myself and leave you to tidy up in the morning."

"Very good."

Also, the man did not my lord him every time he opened his mouth.

Since Hortensia had taken the town carriage with her to Half Moon Street and he had not yet ordered a replacement, Piers walked the short distance to the Amberlys' house on Grosvenor Square. Despite lacking a vehicle, he had sent both Ape and Benson ahead of him to mingle with the other servants and keep their eyes and ears open.

As he had planned, the dancing had already begun by the time he arrived, so he made a discreet entrance to the ballroom, welcomed only by his vaguely familiar hostess. A tray of sparkling champagne appeared in front of him like magic, so he helped himself to a glass and strolled on, looking for the principal characters of his drama.

With the aid of his quizzing glass, he found Hortensia on the other side of the room among the dowagers. Maria and Gussie were both dancing, though with whom he had no idea except that their partners were neither Gadsby nor Devon. In fact, Devon was dancing in another set with a different young lady entirely. Gadsby...ah, there was Gadsby, strolling into what was, presumably, the card room, set up in an antechamber off the main ballroom.

"Finding any friends, coz?" came Bertie's mocking voice.

"I wasn't looking for any." Piers let the quizzing glass drop. He smiled slightly. "Present company excepted."

Bertie ignored that, if he even listened. "Heard the aunt let you down yesterday and you had to dine alone."

"Your intelligence is poor," Piers said. "I dined at White's, though why you care is beyond me."

As though his unfriendly tone had finally penetrated, Bertie blinked in some surprise. "Just looking after you, coz," he said mildly. "Don't take a pet."

"I wouldn't dream of it. Tell me, Bertie, do you have duties tomorrow?"

"Military ones?" Bertie asked with a wink. "Not until late in the afternoon. Why? Got a party planned?"

"Just a family one. At eleven of the clock at Petteril House."

"In the morning? After a ball? Dash it, Piers!"

"You don't have to come," Piers said. "But things might be decided without you, and you would not have your say."

Bertie scowled. "What things?"

"Tomorrow morning will be better," Piers said and strolled on.

Occasionally he passed young ladies who fluttered their fans at him, or seated mamas who bowed to him while the young ladies beside them blushed and smiled. To each, Piers bowed distantly, as was his habit, and walked on.

Then it struck him, and he almost laughed aloud. He realized with some astonishment that he was now an eligible bachelor. From the impossibility of a married life at university to a marriage mart catch in one bound. Fate was certainly an amusing mistress.

Not quite so amusing when he considered that it was probably his duty to marry and produce heirs. After all, his father, two male cousins, and an older brother, hadn't been enough to preserve *him* from the title. After Piers, there was only Bertie—who would love to be viscount, admittedly—and any legitimate sons he might bring into the world. Though in the normal way of things, Piers would outlive Bertie who, besides being several years older, was a soldier. Like poor cousin John, Bertie might conceivably be called upon to fight and die for his country.

Perhaps Pier's black amusement was reflected in his face, for one seated young lady actually smiled at him directly and murmured, "Good evening, my lord."

He inclined his head aloofly. "Good evening," he said, and would have passed on had he not he caught a flash of humiliation in her face, quickly veiled, although the sudden twist of her fingers in her lap betrayed anger too.

Damnation. Had she been someone he had encountered at Maria's the other afternoon? This was why he hated such gatherings, because while it was all very well protecting his own dignity, he never truly meant it to be at the expense of anyone else's. Of course, it might have been a ruse on the girl's part to scrape an acquaintance, but from that glimpse of her eyes, he doubted it.

He paused, forcing a smile to his lips. "Forgive me, I was wool gathering. How do you do?"

At this, the older lady beside her, suddenly stopped talking to the person next to her and whisked her attention to him.

"Are you acquainted with my aunt, Mrs. Manners?" the young lady said, looking as if she wanted the floor to swallow her up. "Aunt, this is Lord Petteril."

"Oh, how do you do?" Mrs. Manners beamed at him and gave him her hand, which he bowed over punctiliously. "Of course, you may dance with my niece."

Colour swept over the younger lady's face and neck. "Perhaps a turn about the room, my lord, in search of lemonade," she said in a strangled voice.

Piers could only take pity on her and offer his hand to rise and then his arm.

"I am so sorry," the young lady said in a rush. "I know very well you did not ask me to dance, but my aunt cannot hear in such crowds and makes assumptions. You may leave me just here, if you please."

"Why would I do that?" Piers asked.

"Because you have no idea who I am."

Piers tried a winning smile. "Forgive me. I have a quite shocking memory."

"I suppose it was several years ago, but truly I did not mean to *encroach*. I am Louise Austen. You knew my brother at Oxford."

A light dawned, along with relief of not simply having forgotten her from two days before. "Percy?" he exclaimed. "You are Percy

Austen's sister! Of course!" As Percy's guest, some years ago, he had once spent a week in the same house as her. But she no longer had pigtails or short skirts. "You must admit you have changed."

"I am no judge. I *feel* the same."

"Why, so do I. Even though they keep telling me I'm a viscount now."

She smiled at that, a genuine smile which made her rather pretty. She had a charming widow's peak, giving her face a piquant heart shape that he hoped he would remember in future.

"I have to say you look the part," she said approvingly. "The two quizzing glasses are a particularly good touch. Are they for quelling the pretensions of those you find offensive?"

"You mean like this?" He picked up one glass and, thinning his lips, mimed displeasure with a student who had failed his examination twice from lack of study. Then, as someone walked across his line of vision, he dropped it hastily.

Miss Austen laughed. "Exactly like that!"

"It would be fun, but mostly I use them for seeing." Having discovered a tray of lemonade, he presented her with a glass. "How is Percy? Is he with you in London?"

"Sadly, not. He remains in Dorset, though he may come to town later in the Season."

At that moment, Haggs strolled up to join them. Piers performed the introductions and Haggs was as delighted as he to encounter Percy Austen's sister.

Over the next few minutes, Piers began to realize that not all conversation at parties had to be dull and that he was being distracted from his mission of looking after his cousin Gussie. When Haggs invited Miss Austen to dance, Piers effaced himself and used his quizzing glass once more to locate the various members of his family.

Gussie was dancing once more, with another young man Piers did not recognize. Devon stood with a group of laughing people close by, but he was not even looking at Gussie who, if anything, seemed somewhat piqued. Although she laughed up at her partner, as though he was the most entertaining man in the world, there were spots of hectic colour in her cheeks, and the sparkle in her eyes did not look like that of a young lady enjoying herself.

While the dance went on, Piers explored the exits. The ballroom had been built onto the back of the house, so besides the way he had come in, straight through the entrance hall from the front, there were French windows opening on to a small, lit terrace at the back. Only one door had been left ajar to let in some cool air, for it was still too early in the year for even the best evening to be anything but chilly. Piers made use of it and wandered out on to the terrace.

He was alone there, despite the lanterns, which showed him a carved wooden bench and a couple of steps leading down from one side of the terrace to a path through a small kitchen garden, beyond which was the mews. Presumably Ape and Benson lurked out there, unless they were in the kitchen. There were certainly a few lights coming from the mews, but they showed him no waiting carriages.

Going back through the ballroom, he walked out through the entrance hall as though seeking the cloakroom. A footman stood at attention by the front door, ready to open it for him. Clearly, no more guests were expected to arrive.

"Just a few seconds to get a breath of air," Piers said to the footman. In the square, a carriage moved smartly into Brook Street. Apart from that, all was quiet. He turned back into the house, acknowledging he could easily be wrong that Devon would make some kind of move tonight. The man could easily wait until after the ball, or early tomorrow morning or even the day after. And Piers doubted he could keep a very close watch on either Devon or Gussie all that time.

His original aim had been to let Devon show Gussie what a weasel he was. But he might have to change that plan and simply scare Devon off.

Ambling back to the ballroom, Piers positioned himself so that when the dance ended, he could encounter Gussie as if by chance. Her discontented gaze caught him, and immediately she smiled with apparent sincerity. "You came! How delightful. Allow me to introduce Mr. Bronson. Sir, my cousin, Lord Petteril."

The men exchanged bows.

"So, you are relieved of your duty, Mr. Bronson," Gussie told him, abandoning her swain's arm for Piers's. "My cousin will return me to my sister."

"To Maria," Piers murmured as they abandoned the disconsolate Mr. Bronson, "not your mama?"

"Well, one or the other. Maria said Mama does not pay enough attention, which is true, though I have to admit to avoiding her on occasions. Who is that lady with Mr. Devon?"

"I have no idea," replied Piers, who had deliberately led her past him. Devon appeared to be about to dance with the young lady in question. "Do you mind?"

"Not in the slightest," Gussie said grandly. "Why should I?"

"I have no idea," Piers said. "He seems a little...ordinary for you."

She blinked up at him. "*Ordinary?* Do you really think so? I found him quite amusing."

"Some people are. For a little. They don't always remain amusing."

She appeared to think about that, then her eyes narrowed. "He has not even asked me to dance. Not once!"

"Well, don't look at me. I don't dance. And here is Maria."

Maria acknowledged her sister and Piers with a nod. Although surrounded by a court of admirers herself, she seemed at least to have taken his warning about Gussie seriously. As Gussie went off to dance again with one of Maria's court, Piers saw that there would be no opportunity to invite her discreetly to his "family party" tomorrow morning. After a few minutes' conversation, he wandered off to the card room in search of her husband.

For once, Sir Jeremy Gadsby appeared to be winning, which put him in an excellent mood.

"Greetings, Petteril!" he said as soon as he caught sight of his wife's cousin. "I've just finished here, so if you want my place...?"

"Oh, no, just observing." He bowed cooly in the vague direction of the other players and turned back to Gadsby. "But while I've caught you, I'd appreciate your presence—and Maria's—tomorrow morning at Petteril House. Shall we say eleven?"

Gadsby laughed. "We most certainly shall not. Say two. Won't be up until midday."

"Make an exception," Piers said, tucking a card into Gadsby's pocket. It had the date and time written clearly across it. "I'll be sure to let Maria know, too." He strolled away leaving Gadsby unsure whether to be amused or annoyed.

Gussie's feelings toward Henry Devon had grown somewhat ambiguous. But she was thoroughly incensed by his totally ignoring her at the Amberlys' ball after making such a fuss about dancing with her there. She was aware that the spikes of jealousy in her heart were at least half anger, but she seemed powerless to deal with them.

Even flirting as blatantly as she dared with all her dance partners failed to make her feel better. Or attract Henry's notice. Even the knowledge that she might have captured the interest of one of her sister's erstwhile devotees, did not prevent Henry's handsome, teasing face from filling her mind's eye.

But then, just when she had given up hope, and was being escorted back to Maria before the supper dance, there he was in front of her, with two glasses, not of lemonade, but champagne. She was forced to halt or swerve around him. Her escort chose the former for her.

"Miss Withan," Henry said, smiling broadly. "I thought you would enjoy refreshment before our dance."

"I don't recall granting you a dance, Mr. Devon."

"If I were not holding two glasses, I should clutch my wounded heart. Have pity on me, Loxley."

Gussie's escort laughed and traitorously abandoned her. Gussie hesitated, swinging between temper and desire, and eventually snatched the proffered glass.

"Don't be angry," Henry said softly. "I have been throwing your family off the scent."

"What scent?" she demanded.

"Come onto the terrace and I shall tell you."

"I have no wish to go onto the terrace. It is much too cold."

"You won't be cold when you're dancing."

"Dancing?" she repeated, intrigued in spite of herself. "On the terrace?"

His eyes held hers now, working all their old magic, as he leaned closer. "You told me you wanted to waltz," he whispered. "We can't do it inside, can we?"

Excitement sparked. "What if someone else is there?" she asked, unable to prevent herself glancing toward the French windows.

"Shall we go and see?"

"Why not?" she said recklessly.

She was right. The evening *was* too cold to be comfortable. But when he threaded his arm through hers so that they could touch while sipping from their glasses, she forgot all about the temperature. Then he took her glass from her and set it beside his somewhat precariously on the balustrade. The music began inside, and Henry took her in his arms.

The waltz was a simple, turning dance, but strangely exhilarating when held so close to a handsome man in the moonlight. Henry smiled, quite his old, delightful self as he guided her across the terrace, turning often enough to make her pleasantly dizzy and even lean daringly against him. He danced amusingly down the steps and then, somehow, she was running with him hand-in-hand through the darkness.

Abruptly, she pulled back. "Wait! I don't want to go further. Take me back!"

When he only tugged her onward, she yanked her hand free, glaring at him in anger that he should treat her so. But before she could speak, he simply seized her round the waist, sweeping her right off the ground and over the garden gate into an entirely different set of arms. She was so startled that her scream was silent, and as she saw the waiting carriage only yards away, fear swept over her like a tide.

Chapter Twelve

Ape was pretty bored, kicking his heels among the Amberlys' grooms. They let him pet the horses and treated him with amiable contempt. Mr. Benson circled mostly around the front of the house.

"Why don't you look after your own horses, then?" one of the younger grooms asked Ape.

"It's cold out there. We've left the carriage on the other side of the square rather than go home and have to get the horses out again. His lordship won't stay that late, and we'd rather be ready." It was the story they had concocted, and it earned the scorn it deserved from the other grooms.

As though ashamed, Ape stuck his head out of the stable door, and at last saw a carriage making its slow, silent way along the mews. A flash of light showed a yellow painted chaise. A hired post-chaise! His lordship was right about tonight.

The chaise came to a halt several yards from the Amberlys' stable and the gate leading to the back of the house. In the dark, Ape made out the shape of the postilion astride the lead horse. And loping past it, the figure of another man. Benson.

Ape was about to go and meet him when someone else moved out of the darkness and brushed past him. The light spilling from the ballroom and the stables must have illuminated Ape as it did Henry Devon's valet, for the man stopped suddenly and frowned at him.

"Here. Why do I keep seeing your face wherever I go?"

"'Cause you're lucky," Ape grinned. "Don't recall yours, though."

"Why you hanging about here?"

"Waiting for my master."

"Who's your master, then?"

"None of your business," Ape said, and the man seized his elbow.

"Let the boy go," Benson said, looming out of the darkness.

"Or what?" the valet sneered.

Benson nodded toward the stable full of grooms, who were all advancing, flatteringly prepared to stand up for Ape.

The valet all but shoved Ape away and marched on his way toward the waiting chaise. As one, Ape and Benson stepped back toward the stable, as though they weren't interested, but Ape saw the valet speaking to the postilion.

"I'd better get himself," Ape murmured.

Benson said, "Go the kitchen and send a footman up to get him. I'll watch the carriage."

Ape jumped lightly over the gate and ran up the path toward the music and the light. Abruptly, he pushed himself further into the shadows because someone was on the terrace. Two people, dancing in each other's arms in the lantern light. Ape peered closer. It was *them*, Devon and Miss Gussie, spinning across the terrace and down the few steps to the garden.

Ape flattened himself against the trunk of an apple tree, but neither even glanced at him. Gussie, who had been laughing softly, seemed now to be furious. As Devon dragged her along with him, she flung herself backward to pull free. But Devon only grabbed her bodily, and Ape knew he had run out of time.

He ran straight toward the terrace.

Piers had just noticed with a certain amount of satisfaction that Percy's sister, Miss Austen, appeared to be a wallflower no longer, when his cousin Maria suddenly seized him by the arm.

Dragged away from the background conversation ranging from crop rotations to Napoleon Bonaparte, to unrest in the north, Piers regarded his cousin with some surprise.

"Where is Gussie?" she demanded.

"Gussie?"

"Augusta! I can't find her. I've been doing my best to watch her, I really have, but she is not dancing, and she is not with Mama." There was genuine anxiety in her eyes that suddenly ratcheted up his own. "*And* I don't see Devon."

"See if she's with your mother, then look in all the alcoves and cloakrooms," Piers said grimly. On his way toward the French windows, he caught Haggard by the shoulder and dragged him back from his group of friends. "I need you to go to the front of the house and if you see my cousin Gussie, bring her back. Otherwise, help Maria."

He didn't wait to see the result of his mutterings—he trusted Haggs—but slipped through the open door onto the terrace.

At once his arm was seized and he found himself gazing down at the unmistakable face of his tiger.

"He's just dragged her off into the mews," Ape said urgently. "There's a yellow bounder waiting there."

Piers didn't hesitate but jumped the balustrade into the garden and ran, Ape at his heels.

Gussie, passed from person to person over the gate like a parcel, finally opened her mouth to scream.

"Please don't," whispered a voice. "I won't hurt you. Trying to rescue you."

Light from the nearby stable fell across the speaker's face, a plain middle-aged face framed by short, greying hair, and the clothing of a groom. As though to prove his point, the man set her on the ground and stood in front of her, fists raised.

"You're not Larson!" Henry's indignant voice burst out. "Larson!"

Although she felt quite comfortingly secure behind the groom, whoever he was, curiosity always got the better of Gussie and she stepped to the side to see better.

At once, Henry lunged toward her. But at the same time, two figures leapt over the gate to the Amberlys' garden. Piers and his tiger.

With astonishing speed, Piers lashed out with his fist, connecting loudly, and Henry staggered across the lane. As the valet flew at Piers in retaliation, the tiger stuck out his foot and tripped him, which enabled Piers to catch him off balance and hurl him into the furiously advancing figure of Devon.

"Cor," the tiger said with undisguised admiration. "I didn't know you could fight two of 'em at once."

"Of course he can," Gussie said shakily. "He grew up with a big brother and lots of bigger cousins. They weren't always kind."

"Neither am I," Piers said, reaching down and hauling Devon to his feet by the front of his elegant coat. Benson stood over the valet while a lot of other men seemed to have spilled out of the stable and surrounded them.

Piers released Henry's coat. "I believe you owe my cousin an apology."

Henry tried to bluster. "My lord, you have entirely misunderstood the—"

"Apology," Piers interrupted. He didn't even sound fierce, just implacable. Which was interesting, for he had always seemed too amiable, too polite to be implacable.

Henry swallowed, trying to straighten his coat, and ease the cravat that must suddenly have felt too tight. "Of course, I apologise for any distress caused to Miss—"

"And your word that you will make no effort to see her again unless she sends for you," Piers said.

Henry glanced at him, a hopeful gleam in his eye as he imagined he saw a way out. Gussie was disgusted. What in the world had she ever seen in such a pathetic weasel?

"Of course. My word as a gentleman," he said humbly.

"Good. Perhaps you will remember that, from your lands away up in the north, which I believe require your attention quite urgently."

Gussie regarded Piers in some surprise. "They do?"

"You're rumbled," the tiger told Henry with some glee. "I don't suppose you want the truth spread about."

"Go and *do* something," Piers said. "I believe your post chaise awaits."

"It's already got his luggage in it," the groom remarked.

"Goodbye then," Piers said, turning his back on Henry and offering his arm quite casually to Gussie. "Cousin?"

Gussie's hand was shaking as she laid it on Pier's arm. Delayed emotion threatened to bubble up and shatter her. But through the disappointment, the shame, and the pain of an illusory first love lost forever—and good riddance—she was conscious of relief. The fear had gone, and she *knew* that Piers, the cousin so despised by her family, was worth a thousand of Henry Devon.

"Thank you," she whispered.

"There is no need," Piers said. "If you really want to thank anyone, make it Ape, here. He was the one who noticed that Devon frightened you."

Ape, which was the very odd name of Piers's equally odd tiger, opened the gate for her. She paused to look at him, frowning, then up at Piers. "I wasn't frightened of him!" Then she recalled the brief struggle in the gloom of Petteril House, and the subsequent feelings of discomfort that mingled with the excitement he had told her she should feel—and did to some extent. She hadn't trusted him anymore. And that was a form of fear.

She walked quickly through the gate, saying in a rush, "For a dare, I took the keys to Petteril House and showed it to Henry when we should have been driving in the park. It wasn't the first time. We dared each other several times. Once we drove out of the park and galloped up the Edgeware Road, dodging carts and carriages and people by the dozen... But in your house, it was different. He...he..." She broke off, unable to find the words.

"All hands?" Ape said behind her.

And she actually smiled over her shoulder at the boy before she realized what she was admitting to a stranger, a servant. God, he shouldn't even have been listening. As though he understood—or perhaps Piers glared at him—the tiger fell back and melted into the shadows.

"I felt childish not to like being pawed," she confided. "But I was flattered, too. I suppose you don't understand that, and why should you? I was so stupid. I was even jealous to see him dancing with other women and ignoring me."

Piers led her onto the empty terrace and to a bench under a lantern.

"Am I fit to be seen?" she asked ruefully.

"You will be." He seemed to be closely examining her hair, which felt loose, and some locks had definitely tumbled down around her neck. He began to collect pins from the fallen bits.

"What if we are seen?" she asked nervously.

"It's the supper dance. Those not dancing will be raiding the buffet tables early. The rest will charge after them as soon as is polite."

"You make it sound like a schoolboy riot."

"Well, the Oxford balls were a little like that. I expect tonnish people behave better."

She eyed him, but all his concentration was on her hair, threading, rolling, pinning. "You say that even after this evening?"

"Devon is not everyone. I *am* correct in believing you never will summon him?"

She shuddered. "Never. Not if my life depended on it."

"It never will. You have family to call on if you are in trouble."

She was silent a moment. "I think Maria knew. She never paid me much attention before."

"Everyone gets caught up in their own little bits of life. It doesn't mean they don't want to help, just that they haven't noticed it's necessary. There." He stood back and examined her from several angles.

Much struck, she blurted, "Maria isn't happy, either, is she?"

"Seems to me, none of you are very happy. Give me your dancing slippers and I'll see if I can brush off the worst."

She bent and obliged. "Are you?"

She could not see his face for shadow, and there was a definite pause before he answered lightly, "Happy? Of course. I am the viscount, am I not?"

"You are an excellent viscount, and I probably shouldn't ask where and how you learned to dress a lady's hair."

"I am observant."

"Being so clever," she said, with the glimmerings of a genuine smile.

"And the viscount," he reminded her, handing her back the slippers. "I doubt you'll be able to wear them in the future, but you should get away with the rest of the evening."

"You are rather wonderful, Piers," she said, her voice suddenly unsteady again. She swallowed. "Was it all about money? With Henry? Is that what you meant about repairing his estates? Is he a fortune hunter after all?"

He took her hand, raising her to her feet. "I believe so. Your mother was not the only one taken in by Lady Sindon's correspondence. And Devon went out of his way to lie about his family wealth." He placed her hand on his arm but stood a moment longer looking down at her. "But I am not talking about money at all when I say you are worthy of so very much better than a Henry Devon."

It was a silly time to discover that Piers was so handsome as well as wonderful. She could not even speak the words for the emotion clogging her throat. But she smiled at him mistily and let him lead her back inside the ballroom.

Catching sight of his grazed knuckles at the ballroom door, Piers hastily dug his gloves from his coat pocket and pulled them on.

"Oh dear," Gussie said with a mix of amusement and distress. "Where are you taking me? To Mama?"

"To supper," he said. "This is the supper dance."

"You won't tell Mama about this, will you?"

He hesitated, then sighed. "Not tonight. But I will have to. Don't worry, though. I'll do it in such a way as you will be in no trouble at all."

He didn't expect her to believe that for a moment—he wasn't sure *he* believed it—but rather to his surprise she nodded. In the supper room, he found Haggs had taken Maria in already.

"Gussie!" Maria exclaimed, relief standing out in her face for a brief, almost naked moment. "I was so afraid something had happened to you."

"Abducted by pirates," Piers said flippantly, handing Gussie into the chair beside her sister.

"All well?" Haggs asked casually, although his eyes were serious,

"Quite well," Piers replied. "Mr. Devon has gone home early. He was not well."

Gussie giggled and Piers thought that was the best sign possible.

Dismissed with a flick of his lordship's eyes, Ape fell back and watched them go on alone. He didn't know why he'd even followed them, except that he had felt part of the adventure. But if anything was guaranteed to remind him of his place, it was the sight of Lord Petteril and his lady

cousin walking together back to the ballroom they had left only minutes before.

For no reason. Ape's throat constricted. Something ached so hard
he wanted to cry. Only he wouldn't, because boys didn't cry, and in any
case, he had nothing to cry about. From penniless and starving, surviv-
ing on the streets with the odd night under cover at the Silver Jug, at
the beck and call of thieves and men of all sorts of nefarious intent, he
now had a proper job with horses, working for a decent, rich man, with
other servants who were even kind to him. He was learning to read. He
could already write his own name, after a fashion, and he could be head
groom one day. He had got out of St. Giles and would stay out.

If he kept his secret. All his secrets. What if other grooms arrived
to work and slept in the stables, too? Sooner or later, they'd notice that
he never undressed, washed or relieved himself in front of them. The
damnable monthly bleedings would give him away when he couldn't
run off and hide for the few days until it stopped. But maybe he could
last a year, learn lots and move on with a glowing character from Lord
Petteril.

But he didn't like the thought of moving on. It made him feel empty, even worse than watching his lordship walk off with Miss Gussie,
knowing he, Ape, could never be on those kinds of terms with him.
Never for longer than the odd moment when his lordship forgot.

He found himself in the mews beside Mr. Benson.

"Has he gone?" Ape asked, meaning Devon.

Benson smiled with considerable satisfaction. "He has. Taken the
slimy valet with him."

"Did they take the yellow bounder?"

Benson was positively grinning now. "They did. I think his lordship—and the poor young lady—has seen the last of him. Hides his
light under a bushel, our lord, don't he?"

"What do you mean?" Ape asked suspiciously, ready to defend on
the instant.

"Well, he's all mild and polite, then turns up damned handy with his fives. That was quite a wisty caster!"

Ape grinned too at the memory. "Man of parts, his lordship."

"Well, I won't be getting on the wrong side of him," Benson said happily. "Come on, let's go home and get a cup of tea from Mrs. Gale before bed."

Chapter Thirteen

Although his lordship had not come home terribly late from the Amberly ball, and had, in fact, ridden out shortly after dawn, nobody in the kitchen really expected him to be up to reading lessons in the library.

"'Course he is," Ape scoffed. "I'm going up as usual. If he ain't there, well I've only wasted a minute of my day finding out."

The other readers went with him, mainly to prove him wrong, Ape suspected, but there was his lordship as usual, perfectly attired, seated at the head of the large library table. Admittedly, he was not reading, for once, but gazing at nothing, so deep in thought that when he noticed their arrival it seemed to startle him.

However, he bade them briskly to come in and sit, and from then on, the lesson proceeded as normal. Everyone read a short sentence from the book in front of them and his lordship looked as proud as if they were his own children. Ape felt a flood of warmth toward him that didn't go away, even later when Petteril came to view the sentence he had written and corrected the form of one of his letters. Ape just liked the fact that he could smell him when he leaned so close. A clean smell, of soap and skin and goodness that made his heart flutter with gratitude.

Not that his lordship was ever *friendly* during the lessons. He was patient, but entirely impersonal, his manner exactly the same to each of his pupils.

Only when they were all filing out at the end did he say with odd abruptness, "Ape, I need a word with you."

Obediently, Ape hung back, but with a certain dread dragging at his heels. He didn't like his lordship's tone, or the faint frown lurking between his brows. His posture was wrong too, stiff and uneasy. A man with something unpleasant to say. Or do.

Oh no, not now...

Ape stood in the centre of the room, as rigid as Petteril, as though pretending to be the perfect servant. *Always pretending...*

"Damn it, Ape, sit down," Lord Petteril growled, throwing himself into one of the easy chairs by the fireplace, and waving his hand commandingly toward the other.

Warily, Ape walked forward and perched on the edge of the chair.

Lord Petteril scowled at him. "There is no easy way to say this, so I'm just going to be brutal."

Ape sprang back up. "You don't need to. I'll go."

Petteril blinked. "Go where?"

"What do you care?" Ape demanded.

Petteril stared at him, but he looked more baffled than angered by such unforgivable rudeness. Unexpectedly, a rueful smile tugged at his lips. "Conversations with you never go the way I expect. I am not dismissing you. I am acknowledging a problem that *you* have to think about."

Ape scowled. "What problem?" he asked, still too aggressively because he was afraid to believe he wasn't being dismissed.

"The problem that you are not and never have been a boy."

The blood drained from Ape's face so fast that his ears sang. "You been at the brandy, mister?"

"Oh, stop it," Petteril snapped. "Don't you think you owe me honesty?"

It hit Ape like a blow, knocking him so far off balance that he grasped at the arm of the chair at his back. "I *give* you honesty," he said desperately. "I been a boy so long that's how I am, how I think of myself. I want to be a boy. A girl's no use to you. You don't need to treat me any different."

His lordship looked wearily patient, which cut him to the quick. He had never looked at Ape like that before, only at those who disappointed him. "You can't hide it forever. It isn't safe. What do you think is going to happen to you when someone other than me discovers the truth? Do you want to be sleeping in a stable with a lot of lads when it comes out that you're a girl? Do you want some gentlemen to notice? To decide rules of decency—which barely extend to servants in many cases—don't apply to females who have already broken them by wearing breeches?"

Ape closed his eyes. He had a horrible feeling he was going to cry. "I been a boy for years," he whispered. "It's *me*."

Lord Petteril didn't speak. But elsewhere in the house there were voices, loud ones, shrill ones, and they were coming this way. Ape's eyes flew open again. His lordship swore under his breath and sprang to his feet just as the library door burst open, Francis the footman was all but knocked aside and the Dowager Lady Petteril sailed into the room, the rest of the family at her heels.

Like a stately galleon of old, Piers thought savagely, *surrounded by tugs and fishing boats*.

"I am sorry, my lord," Park's voice somehow cut through the wall of noise coming from his family. "I was showing her ladyship to the drawing room as you had requested."

Piers lifted his quizzing glass, and in the sudden silence surveyed his aunt, triumphant rather than ashamed. Gadsby and Bertie deigned to be amused, though Gadsby yawned, and Bertie's eyes had developed that cruel, happy gleam Piers remembered from childhood bullying. Maria had the decency to look uneasy, and Gussie indignant.

And poor little Ape in the midst of distress none of them would ever think about.

"Rude," Piers observed, the one word like a gunshot through the silence. It had worked for him in the past, in a room full of boisterous students. Perhaps Hortensia perceived the truth of it. Certainly, a hint of colour mottled her face though her chin lifted under his scrutiny.

Piers let the glass fall. "Ape, you may go. We shall finish our conversation later. In all courtesy and in deference to my aunt's age, it seems I must change the order of my appointments."

Hortensia gasped. Bertie gave a shocked gasp of laughter.

"Will there be anything else, my lord?" Park inquired loftily.

"Thank you, no," Piers said, denying his family the refreshment they no doubt felt they deserved.

As Park bowed and departed, Bertie lounged across the doorway and Ape slipped around the walls with her head down. Piers's heart ached for her, adding to his fury with his family for interrupting. He did not want her suffering more than she had, especially not uncertainties which could, after all, feel worse than anything concrete.

"Please, sit," he said, his impatient hand barely courteous as he waved it to the various chairs around the room. "The library hardly has the space and comfort of the drawing room, but since you prefer it, enjoy."

"Piers, I don't care for your manner," Hortensia said, sinking into the chair Ape had so briefly occupied."

"I don't care for yours, aunt," Piers said tiredly. "Yet here we are."

Her jaw actually dropped, which gave Gadsby the chance to speak. "What's it about, Petteril?" he asked, swinging a chair around from the table for his wife, and another for himself. Gussie perched on the arm of her mother's chair. "Not the wretched necklace again? It's gone and I'm afraid you will have to live with that."

Piers turned to his desk and took the necklace from the top drawer where he had placed it as soon as it had been delivered earlier in the morning, "This necklace?" he asked mildly, holding it up.

"You found it!" Hortensia exclaimed, while Piers looked around all the other faces to judge their expressions.

"I did," Piers said, "though it cost me some effort. And yet more money."

"So, it was never stolen after all?" Bertie sneered from the doorway. "You are an idiot, Piers."

"Of course it was stolen," Piers said impatiently. "It's what you all do best. Bertie, why are you standing there like a sentry? You'd be better back at your barracks. Shut the door if you're staying so that I don't have to shout the iniquities of our family for the delectation of the rest of the world."

He caught a glimpse of Ape against the bookshelves, her eyes wide with surprise at his manner. He hadn't really wanted her to see his viscount-in-a-pet, but hopefully she would creep out, now that Bertie had closed the door, and join the rest of the servants.

"What iniquities?" Bertie demanded contemptuously, throwing himself into a chair by Maria. "Are you accusing one of us of stealing? From *you*?"

Piers closed his fist around the necklace and sighed. "One of you? No. You have *all* been stealing from me one way or another since my uncle died. Creeping into Petteril House, taking what you want whether it belongs to me or not." He regarded Hortensia who glared back, Maria who dropped her eyes, and Gussie, who blushed and mouthed, *Sorry*. "That has ended, as have the accounts you made use of at Tattersall's, Weston's, Hoby's and the rest. The estate does not thrive and I'm damned if I'll put the rents up so you can live above your means and game what's left of the family fortunes away."

Bertie and Gadsby had turned red and pale respectively, exchanging uneasy glances.

In perfect character, Bertie began to bluster. "Now see here, you jumped up little—"

"I *beg* your pardon?" Piers didn't even resort to the quizzing glass, but it was Bertie's eyes that fell. "Let us be plain, my loving family. You have suffered losses and grief. So have I. I am the last person you wished to inherit the viscountcy, and frankly, it's the last thing *I* wanted. But here I am, grown up and living with it. Which is what *you* will have to do. You have no reason to respect me—though none to disrespect me either. If you wish to acknowledge me, you will at least preserve the courtesies in my house. If you don't, just stay away. I don't much care."

He seemed to have reduced them to silence, but by God he still had their attention. It was quite like giving a lecture, really.

Hortensia recovered first, giving a resentful sniff. "I hardly think it is your place to give me—or any of us!—lessons in adult behaviour."

"Do you not? Is that why your daughter was almost abducted under your nose last night? Why you have been pushing her into the arms of an amoral fortune hunter without making the least enquiry as to his character or circumstances? None of you, not her brother-in-law nor her cousin who imagines he's the real head of the family, bothered to look into him because it was easier to believe he was rich, and would open Gussie to being tapped for your trivial debts."

"What?" Hortensia glared at him and clutched Gussie's hand. "What is he talking about? Gussie?"

"She'll explain later, but the fault is not hers. She is seventeen years old. Allow me to explain what I have done concerning the rest of you. Mr. Pepper will be here at eleven, to make the necessary arrangements, but since you are so early..."

He swept his gaze around them. "Gussie's dowry remains intact, of course. Aunt, you are perfectly entitled to the house you have chosen, if not to all the art and furnishings from Petteril House that you have chosen to fill it with. You may keep them. I will not, however, be paying for your servants, your food or your clothing. Your jointure is more than adequate for these things."

Hortensia's mouth was opening and closing like that of a landed fish. Piers moved on to Gadsby.

"Maria has her own marriage settlements, made by my uncle. You have no other claim on me." He shifted his gaze to Bertie. "Neither do you. I will continue the allowance my uncle chose to make you, but there will be no more."

Gadsby had the grace to look ashamed, wriggling in his seat and casting furtive looks at Maria. Bertie, unused not to dominating a scene, could not yet give up.

He stood up, strolling toward Piers. "You *have* taken a pet, haven't you? Why don't you just calm down and stop throwing accusations around like water?"

"A *pet*?" Piers repeated thoughtfully. "Yes, I suppose I have. You see, although I have not lived much in your fashionable world, I am not used to being regarded as quite so blind or stupid. Nor to being robbed by those who regard themselves as gentlemen."

Bertie took a step closer, his fists clenching, his eyes furious. The eyes of a bullying boy who has never had to grow up. Piers held his gaze and didn't much care if his cousin tried to hit him or not. "Not honourable, Bertie."

Bertie's right arm moved and was still. He didn't step back but his eyes fell.

"What about this wretched necklace?" Hortensia said querulously, no doubt to draw the attention from her favourite nephew. "Where *did* you find it?"

"In bits," Piers said, looking around them all once more. He took the chair by the fireplace and crossed his legs so that he looked comfortable when he was not. In fact, he had weighed talking to the culprit privately, but he was tired of their secrets and their apparent belief that nothing was real if you did not speak of it. "The rubies were in Ellis the

Jeweller's on Ludgate Hill. The rest arrived here by post in a little parcel, with very pretty stones made of glass." Piers opened his palm once more and regarded the necklace.

So did Gadsby, frowning. "The stones are fake?"

"Oh, no, these ones are not. I asked Golding to replace the paste stones with the genuine rubies which I retrieved from Ellis."

"Perhaps Papa did it for extra funds and then forgot," Gussie said, anxious but somewhat lame. "I believe it's not uncommon when people are trying to save face."

"Your father would never have done such a thing!" Hortensia exclaimed.

"No, I don't think he would," Piers agreed, swivelling his attention to her. "But you would."

"I?" Hortensia gasped, outrage. "I did no such thing!"

"Only because someone had beaten you to it. It's why you came here before you knew I had arrived. Your claim of wanting the necklace for Gussie at the Amberly ball was not true."

"But you'd taken it first!" Hortensia accused. "To pay for your fashionable new clothes and your smart horses—"

"Oh, those things are accounted for and not unreasonable expenses for Lord Petteril's precious dignity," Piers said. "You may keep the town carriage, by the way."

Hortensia understood exactly what he meant. He needed a means of getting around town since she had taken the carriage and the horses that were in fact his. He didn't belabour the point.

"So, who *did* take the necklace?" Gussie asked curiously. "We all had keys, you know, at one time or another."

"Yes. I do know. I did wonder if you had taken it for a dare, or if Devon had for his own reasons. But I don't believe either of you knew of the secret compartment in the safe." His eyes focused on Bertie. "*You* did, for you were shown it at the same time as I. And God knows you need the money."

Bertie's lip curled. "You may not like me, Petteril—"

"No, I don't," Piers agreed. "But I acquit you of this crime if only because you regarded the necklace, like the rest of the estate, as your own by right. You wouldn't destroy such a thing, even for money. But you've certainly sold other items from the house that one could not regard as heirlooms. You all have."

"A measly snuff box," Gadsby muttered, reddening. "I'll pay you back."

"It will take you a long time, together with what I had to pay to get the rubies back."

Gadsby jerked upright, staring. "I didn't take your damned rubies!"

"No, but your wife did."

Chapter Fourteen

All eyes swivelled in stunned surprise to Maria, who turned had turned very white.

She lifted her chin, and met Piers's gaze directly, not with defiance but with defeat. "I was hiding behind the curtains when Papa showed you boys how the safe worked. Mama left the keys to Petteril House in my drawing room by accident one day. So, I came and took the necklace. No one liked it. I thought no one would notice if the rubies were replaced with glass. But you came too early and noticed it was gone."

"You gamble genteelly at the houses of fashionable ladies of an afternoon," Piers said. His eye was caught by the slight figure of Ape, sliding out of the library door and quietly closing it behind him. Her. Damn, he hadn't realized she was still in the room.

He glanced back to Maria, "Ladies like Caroline Jeffries, of whom I have heard much talk since I arrived in London. Like the rest of the family, you lose and regard the losses as debts of honour." *Unlike stealing from me or the estate.* "I expect Aunt Hortensia discovered the fact and decided to bail you out. That's the real reason she came for the necklace."

"Only I had already taken it," Maria said flatly.

Her mother remained uncharacteristically silenced, tight-lipped, almost frozen. But Gadsby rose, turning to stare at his wife. "Why did you not come to me? In God's name, Maria—"

"How could I?" Maria burst out. "You cannot pay your own debts! I watch it eating you up every day! How could I add mine to your worries?"

There was pain, genuine feeling between them that perhaps Piers would care about later, but for now, he had had enough.

He rose to his feet, tired of his own emotions and theirs and wanting only to be away from them. "I will pay both your debts for now, but you will pay me back every quarter for that money and for the rubies until you have returned what you owe. If you want my advice, which I know you do not—any of you—stop gambling and stand on your own dashed feet. I am not your golden goose or your private bank. You will excuse me now. I have matters to attend to. Good morning."

He walked between their stunned, silent faces and out of the door which he left open. "Francis, show my guests out," he instructed the footman on the way past.

He knew where to find Ape. Encountering Benson in the mews, where he was polishing the curricle to a commendable shine, Piers lifted his eyebrows.

Benson jerked his head to the stable and Piers went in. It was gloomy after the bright spring sunshine, but he made out Ape at once. She was in the open stall with the Professor, her face buried in the horse's neck. She didn't move when he entered, but she knew he was there for her body stiffened almost imperceptibly.

Piers had never felt so helpless in his life. He could not mutter platitudes or *There, there*, not without being despised. He could not touch her. For lack of any other plan, he went and picked up the stool and set it close to the Professor's stall door, then sat on it and waited.

After a few moments, Ape wiped her face surreptitiously on the Professor's neck. The horse turned its head, nudging her with a pretend nip. She stepped back, glaring at Piers as though daring him to comment on the tear stains running through the grime she had somehow attracted since leaving the library.

"Have they gone?" she demanded.

"Yes."

She gave him a cheeky smile and he could only admire her courage. "You showed 'em. Took them apart and told it how it is. Like a hero."

"I was a pompous ass," he said, feeling the blood seep into his face.

"Nah. You're in twig now. How did you know it was Maria? I mean Lady Gadsby."

"It was the only solution that made sense. She had to be the *lovely lady* who sold the rubies to Ellis. Gadsby still had no money to pay his debts. Neither was Bertie splashing it about. Besides, I don't think they'd have been stupid enough to involve any of their ladybirds in such an enterprise. It can give such creatures too much of a hold."

"Could still have been Devon," Ape pointed out. "With or without Gussie."

Piers wrinkled his nose. "Devon would have taken the pearls, too. In any case, it's done with. I've washed my hands of them."

She smiled and sat down in the straw beside him. "No, you haven't."

He sighed. "No, probably not. But for now, I have. I need to go to Wiltshire next week."

Her smile died and her eyes fell. "Neither of us can be who we want, can we?"

"No." After a pause, he said, "In personal terms, it doesn't matter to me if you're a boy or a girl. You're just Ape. I wish one's sex didn't matter in law either, but it does. If it didn't, Maria would be the viscountess and I could be back with my books and my students in Oxford."

"Do you still miss it?"

He considered. "Yes. But I seem to have acquired other interests. Do you miss St. Giles?"

"Christ, no." She kicked out at the side of the Professor's stall, and one of the greys stuck his head over his door. "But I still can't be a girl. I been a boy too long. What the hell would I do in petticoats? You said I ain't lost my job, but a girl can't be a tiger or a groom, can she?"

"I don't know any," Piers said cautiously.

"Then you might as well have left me in St. Giles," she said with sudden violence. "I wish you had because now I know something different and you're taking it away. Hell, what bloody difference does it make here whether I'm a boy or a girl?"

She knew perfectly well, but the resentment stood out in her eyes, lashing him.

"You still have choices in petticoats," he said. "You just have to think about them and tell me what you'd prefer. There's a place for you here in the capacity you choose. Or if you prefer to leave, Haggs has an amiable stepmother who'd take you in."

Ape stared. "As what?"

"A servant, if you wish, to be trained. Or just to keep you safe while you decide."

"Why'd she do that?" Ape jeered. "From the goodness of her heart?"

"Yes. And her fondness for Haggs and his for me."

"You'd pay her to get me off your hands? Or will I have other...duties?"

He held her angry, suspicious glare and smiled a little sadly. "Am I the enemy now, Ape?"

Tears filled her eyes, and she dashed them furiously against her sleeve. "No," she said hoarsely. "You're the only person was ever kind to me for nothing. Except Annie."

Annie the prostitute who'd probably been her only protection before finding a wealthy man to keep her. Ape had probably felt abandoned then, too.

"You're going away," she said shakily.

"You can stay here with Mrs. Park." He took a deep breath, wondering wildly if he was about to say something he would regret. "Or you can come with me. It might be an opportunity for you to change from Ape into...what? April?"

"I used to be April," she said reluctantly. "Can I really come with you?"

"We'll need to plan it."

"And I can stay as I am until then?" she asked eagerly.

"If you want to. Think first."

"I am thinking. Maybe I could be a girl-tiger." She grinned. "You could make 'em fashionable."

"Maybe not in Wiltshire," he said doubtfully. Then, since her face fell, he nudged her. "But it's an idea. I have an appointment with Mr. Pepper, now, but I shall take the greys out after luncheon. After that, you can rummage in the attics if you like."

"For what?" she asked, bewildered.

"Petticoats."

"You are angry with me," Maria said as they walked back to Mount Street.

Jeremy, who realized he had been striding so furiously fast that his wife had to trot to keep up with him, deliberately slowed his pace and placed her hand on his arm.

"I am not angry with you, but with me." Even that felt like a revelation to himself. He felt as if his whole world was in flux, running away from him, and he was glad of Maria's hand in his arm, small but solid and constant. Things had gone stupidly wrong—he had *allowed* them to go stupidly wrong, through selfishness, thoughtlessness, his weakness for any novel amusement that had led him to gamble money he didn't have, spend money on women he didn't want, do one better than Bertie in outsmarting the nonentity who had become Lord Petteril.

Shame filled him for that too, What the hell had he become? *Not honourable*, Petteril had said to Bertie, and it applied to Jeremy just the same. Not honourable at all.

Without his noticing, they had reached their own house. A watchful footman let them in.

"I suppose you are going to the club?" Maria said lightly.

He shook his head. The club was the last place he wanted to be. Actually, he wanted to be here. With her. "Shall we have breakfast?" he asked.

Her smile almost broke his heart. She issued some brief orders, then they went together to the breakfast parlour and sat down.

She said in a rush. "I got in the habit of playing deep with Caroline Jeffries and others. I didn't even enjoy it, really. The thrill of the win was pleasant enough, but after the first time, it was more than outweighed by the awfulness of losing. And knowing I could not pay. I'm sorry. I should not have taken the necklace, nor sold the rubies. In my defence, all I have is that I had mostly forgotten Piers and he did not seem to matter."

"I regarded him the same way," Jeremy said bleakly. "And with less right. But he does matter, and we will pay him back."

Maria nodded. "It will be difficult. But with the debts paid, we may economize. I shan't play anymore."

"Neither shall I..." His breath caught. "Maria, do you *want* to stay in town for the Season?"

"Not particularly."

"Oh, me neither," he said with relief. "I have a sudden longing for clean, country air, tramping the ancestral acres... And we can live much more cheaply there, pay Petteril back a little quicker."

She nodded and he reached across the table to take her hand. She looked up slowly, as if afraid to read his expression.

He swallowed. "I don't know how it came about, when we live in the same house, but I have missed you."

"I've missed you, too," she whispered, clinging to his fingers. "And I think, perhaps, we are better together."

He raised her hand to his lips and then his cheek. "We are. And we will be again."

A smile trembled on her lips. All the old love warmed her eyes, and something new as well. She said, "We owe it to ourselves and each other. And, perhaps, to our children."

He pressed her hand harder to his cheek. "Maria, I do not care about—"

"I have not told you before because I was not sure, though I have been feeling most strange. But the doctor tells me I am with child."

Jeremy stared at her, while the words sank in. And then, without warning, he wept, for all he had done wrong, and all he would do right. And his wife, his love, wept with him.

Toward the end of the afternoon, with all legal and immediate family business taken care of, Piers strolled out of the office and encountered Mrs. Park coming out of the still room.

"Where's Ape?" he asked her, with a trace of unease. He still wasn't quite sure that she would not run.

"Still up in the attic. What on earth is he looking for?"

"Old clothes," Piers said vaguely.

He went upstairs to his own rooms. After hesitating, he turned into the master bedchamber with the balcony, and walked to the window. Deliberately, he opened the doors and stepped out on to the balcony. He didn't look at the long, deadly drop to the flagstones below. Instead, he gazed across the garden and the next row of elegant houses to the greenness of the park beyond and inhaled the fresh air. Well, as fresh as the air ever got in London.

Everywhere had its ups and downs, its beauty and its ugliness. Like himself and everyone else. Including the family who had rejected him so unequivocally.

He had come a long way in just a few days. The world had not ended because he was Petteril. He had made things better and would continue to do so. He had met old friends and new ones and found more purpose than he could ever have imagined among his books and his students.

Was it a good life he had come to?

It could be. That was up to him. But it was his life, and he would keep it.

A swell of compassion filled him for the man who had so nearly jumped, a pity so strong that it brought tears to his eyes. He could forgive himself for that, and for his other mistakes. For he had a hint now of his true strength, and he would not forget it.

Behind him, he heard movement as his valet came in. Piers swallowed and took a deep, steadying breath before he turned. Stewart was heading into the dressing room with an armful of laundered shirts.

"Stewart," Piers acknowledged. "You can bring the rest of my things from the other room when you have a moment. I believe I shall sleep in here from now on."

"Very good, my lord."

He didn't say it was more suitable and for that Piers was grateful. Not because it *wasn't* suitable. It was, but not just for the viscount. For Piers.

Half laughing at himself for such self-absorbed musings, he went out and along the passage to the attic stairs. The other side of the attic was where the maids slept and could only be reached from the servants' stairs. From here, though, he could reach the attic storage space where he had once played with his brother and cousins. That hadn't all been bad either. He missed his brother Ivor and his cousin John. He even missed his cousin George...

He went up to see what Ape had found, making his way through old furniture in Holland covers, traveling trunks, boxes of toys, and chests of clothes that dated back into the last century. Piles of dusty old portraits and other paintings in ornate frames were propped up against walls and pillars.

He heard her before he saw her, a faint murmur of infectious, musical laughter.

She had found a corner at the far end of the attic where two grimy cheval mirrors stood. She must have wiped them in a half-hearted kind of a way because he could see her slightly streaky reflection as well as her person, and the simple joy of dressing up stood out in her face and in every movement. Several gowns were thrown over the back of a chair and Ape herself danced around in a wide-skirted dress made of sky blue silk and acres of lace. It had been designed for hoops and many petticoats, none of which she was wearing, and it should have looked ridiculous, drowning her small, unassuming frame in its finery. The odd thing was, it didn't.

She obviously found it funny, though, for she was laughing at her own reflection as she swayed, arms spread out in graceful motion, curtseying and spinning between the mirrors. Her short, fair hair flopped untidily about her face, which seemed to amuse her even more.

Piers smiled, rejoicing in her wonder and fun, held spellbound by it.

Her femininity hit him in the gut. Slender, sloping shoulders, a long, elegant neck, delicately defined clavicles... She even had a bosom.

Of course she has, imbecile.

The old-fashioned gown showed the curve of her breasts and waist. How did she look so different as a girl?

She didn't, of course. It was all perception. *His* perception, and right now, it scared him witless.

Natural and unaware, she swayed and twirled like a child at play, except she was no child. She was the loveliest creature he had ever seen, inner and outer beauty shining like the sun, her sense of fun and her poor, lost childhood all spilling from her in one glorious moment.

Ashamed and thoroughly appalled, he crept back the way he had come.

How in the name of all that's holy do I deal with this?

He actually laughed aloud as he ran down the stairs. He would deal with it as he was dealing with everything else. As it came. With responsibility, good sense, and appreciation of the ridiculous. And as much panache as he could muster.

And like everything else, it would enrich him.

A Sneek Peek: *Petteril's Corpse* **(Lord Petteril Mysteries, Book 2):**

Lord Petteril gazed up at the sky, calculating how long it would take for the rain to arrive. His horses, beautifully matched greys, shifted restlessly, shaking their heads, bored at standing still so long and, no doubt, looking forward to their next meal. Petteril, who still thought of himself by his Christian name of Piers, knew how they felt.

He sniffed the air, as though he might smell rain approaching, but all he caught was the earthy scent of forests and, somewhere in the distance, a hint of burning wood.

He sighed. "You had better come out," he called to a large rhododendron bush close to the path, nestling between two young elm trees. "Or we'll all get soaked."

The bush moved, leaves fluttering and causing Piers to hope, but otherwise nothing happened.

"Do you need help?" he enquired.

"No," said the bush defiantly.

"Then hurry up. I don't choose to arrive at my ancestral acres in the guise of drowned rat with semi-drowned servant."

Nothing happened. The bush remained still and silent. He could almost imagine it was glaring at him.

Piers sighed. "Ape," he said warningly.

The bush moved and a grumpy figure in a blue calico dress squeezed out between it and the elm tree. Under one arm she clutched a bundle of grey-ish clothing. Her other hand held a scrap of white linen. The dress fitted her shape and height perfectly, though clearly not her mood. She scowled through her tangle of short, golden-fair hair and marched across to the curricle.

Controlling the twitch of his lips, Piers leaned over and stretched down one hand to help her up. She jerked out of his reach, snapping, "I can manage, for Gawd's sake, I been jumping up and hanging onto the back of this thing for weeks."

"Then get on with it," Piers commanded. "Or you'll have to jump up on the back again."

"I'd rather," she muttered, clambering onto the seat beside him with no grace whatsoever, and roundly cursing her skirts. With unnecessary force, she shoved the roll of clothes into the carpet bag at her feet.

Piers handed her a comb from his pocket and took the white, linen cap from her clutching fingers. Ungraciously, she dragged the comb through her locks, and he plonked the cap on her head. She tossed the comb onto the seat between them and with quick, deft fingers, tied the strings beneath her chin.

"I look ridiculous," she muttered.

She didn't. She looked like a sullen, respectable, awkwardly pretty girl of some indeterminate lower class, in an old fashioned dress. Her age could have been anything between sixteen and twenty summers. Ape was April once more,

"You'll do," Piers replied. "If you stop sulking and can avoid challenging the boot boy to a wrestling match."

"Who's the boot boy?" she asked suspiciously.

"I have no idea."

"I could be the boot boy," she said with such regret that he nudged her.

"No, you couldn't. You're a girl."

The trouble was, she had taken on the guise of a boy so long ago that she didn't even think of herself as female anymore. Her skirts irked her, and she walked and talked like Ape, the street urchin she'd been when Piers first encountered her burgling his house some three weeks ago. For reasons that still were not clear to him, he had employed the child in his own stable until he had realized how unsuitable the arrangement was for one neither child nor boy. The only way he had got her to agree to living as a girl again was to promise her she could make the change between London and his country seat of Haybury. Even so, she had stretched it out until the last moment. They were a bare five miles from his house, Haybury Court.

She sniffed. "I won't fit in."

That was probably true. Mrs. Park, his London housekeeper, had managed to civilize her to some degree, but Ape or April, she still tended to swear like a sailor and do what she wanted rather than what she was told.

"It will be an adjustment," he allowed. The thread of an idea was working through his mind, but he would have to meet the staff first and, more to the point, consult Ape—April—once she had stopped sulking.

He flicked he reins, and the horses moved on.

"Can you smell burning?" April asked suddenly.

"Someone burning garden waste. The village is just beyond the wood."

She shook her head, not with impatience but unease that was almost dread. "No, there's more n' wood. It's like...plague."

"Plague!" He stared at her. "What on earth do you mean?"

"Maybe not plague but, you know, sickness. When people get ill, and everyone catches it and loads of 'em die and they have to burn their clothes in—" She broke off, her eyes widening. "That's it. It's burning clothes. Who'd burn clothes if they didn't have plague?"

It made an uneasy kind of sense. April had grown-up in the crowded slums of the east end docks and St. Giles, where bouts of illness were devastating to people already poor, exhausted and malnourished.

Piers sniffed the air again and turned his head into the wind. "It's not in the village either. It's too close."

He pulled up the horses once more and from habit, April jumped down to go to the horses' heads while he alighted. However, without a word, Piers looped the reins around a tree and strode off toward the smoky smell, April at his heels.

"There." She pointed past him to a small clearing, where smoke issued in a lethargic kind of way from an indeterminate heap.

They walked toward it. There was no fire left, only a pile of ash and a few singed, smoking rags. Piers, glancing around the clearing, saw another, much worrying sight only a few feet away. He swerved toward it.

A man, naked as the day he was born, lay face down on the gravelly ground. Quickly, Piers crouched beside him, reaching for his wrist and searching for a pulse, but he already knew he wouldn't find one. The flesh was chillingly cold and stiff and had been dead for some time.

*(Read the rest in **Petteril's Corpse**, available late September 2023)*

About the Author

Mary Lancaster is a USA Today bestselling author of award winning historical romance and historical fiction. She lives in Scotland with her husband, one of three grown-up kids, and a small dog with a big personality.

Her first literary love was historical fiction, a genre which she relishes mixing up with romance and adventure in her own writing. Several of her novels feature actual historical characters as diverse as Hungarian revolutionaries, medieval English outlaws, and a family of eternally rebellious royal Scots. To say nothing of Vlad the Impaler.

More recently, she has enjoyed writing light, fun Regency romances, with occasional forays into the Victorian era. With its slight change of emphasis, *Petteril's Thief*, is her first Regency-set historical mystery.

Connect with Mary on-line – she loves to hear from readers:

Email Mary: Mary@MaryLancaster.com

Website: http://www.MaryLancaster.com

Newsletter sign-up: https://marylancaster.com/newsletter/

Facebook: https://www.facebook.com/mary.lancaster.1656

Facebook Author Page: https://www.facebook.com/MaryLancasterNovelist/

Twitter: @MaryLancNovels https://twitter.com/MaryLancNovels

Bookbub: https://www.bookbub.com/profile/mary-lancaster

Made in United States
Troutdale, OR
08/10/2024

21893044R00094